D0040746

George, Jean Craighead
    The talking earth.   Harper & Row, 1983.
    151 p.

    Billie Wind ventures out alone into the
Florida Everglades to test the legends of
her Indian ancestors and learns the importance of listening to the earth's vital
messages.

9.89   I. Title   LC 82-48850

The Talking Earth

Other Novels by Jean Craighead George

JULIE OF THE WOLVES
Winner of the 1973 Newbery Medal

GOING TO THE SUN

CRY OF THE CROW

THE
TALKING
EARTH

Jean Craighead George

j

c.1

1 8 17

———— HARPER & ROW, PUBLISHERS ————

Cambridge, Philadelphia, San Francisco, London, Mexico, City, São Paulo, Sydney

———————— NEW YORK ————————

Library of Congress Cataloging in Publication Data
George, Jean Craighead, date
    The talking earth.

    Summary: Billie Wind ventures out alone into the
Florida Everglades to test the legends of her Indian
ancestors and learns the importance of listening to the
earth's vital messages.
    [1. Seminole Indians—Fiction.   2. Indians of North
America—Fiction.   3. Everglades (Fla.)—Fiction.
4. Ecology—Fiction]   I. Title.
PZ7.F2933Tal 1983   [Fic]   82-48850
ISBN 0-06-021975-0
ISBN 0-06-021976-9 (lib. bdg.)

Designed by Trish Parcell
10 9 8 7 6 5 4 3 2 1
First Edition

Contents

LOST DOG SLOUGH · 1

THE SERPENT · 17

PETANG · 32

SWAMP TALK · 53

COOOTCHOBEE · 74

SWAMP RIVALS · 88

THE MUTE ONE · 105

OATS · 128

SO SPOKE BURDEN
AND ALL OF THE ANIMALS · 144

Lost Dog Slough

Billie Wind could see the orange tree through the open walls of the council house. A white bird floated down upon it, and she wondered if it had a nest nearby.

"Billie Wind." The medicine man was speaking. "May I have your attention?" She was standing beside her sister Mary in the dim light of the house. Outside the sunlight was white and hot. Inside a soft trade wind blew under the palm-thatched roof, cooling the air pleasantly. Charlie Wind, the medicine man, who was also her uncle and friend, cleared his throat.

"Billie Wind," he repeated. "May I have your attention?" She promptly looked from the bird to the dark eyes of the elderly man.

"It is told that you do not believe in the animal gods who talk." He frowned.

"It is told that you do not believe that there is a great serpent who lives in the Everglades and punishes bad Seminoles." He shook his head, then cast a sober glance at the councilmen, who were seated on the hard earth around him.

"And it is told that you doubt that there are little people who live underground and play tricks on our people." He pulled his white Seminole cape closer around his lean shoulders, forcing Billie Wind to notice that it was too long. It almost touched the black-and-white border of his skirt.

"Are you listening to me?"

"Yes," she answered and smiled, tightening her lips so she would not giggle.

"The council has met. We are disturbed by your doubts."

Billie Wind caught her breath. She knew perfectly well these men did not believe in the serpent and the talking animals and the dwarfs. They were educated and wise men. She knew them well. Several were her uncles, others were the fathers of her best friends. She waited for them to laugh understandingly as they usually did when the old legends and beliefs were discussed.

But they did not even smile. Charlie Wind crossed his arms on his chest.

"We are a tribe of the Seminole Indians," he said in a solemn voice. "We believe that each person is part of the Great Spirit who is the wind and the rain and the sun and the earth, and the air above the earth. Therefore we can not order or command anyone." He paused. "But we do agree that you should be punished for being a doubter."

Billie Wind glanced from face to face, searching for the good humor that would soon end this to-do about serpents and dwarfs. No one smiled, not even her comical uncle, Three-Hands-on-the-Saddle.

"What do you think would be a suitable punishment for you, Billie Wind?"

She let her mind wander, waiting for someone to break the silence and send her off to play. When it became apparent that this would not happen, she concentrated on a punishment: something ridiculous, something they would not let her do, it would be so dangerous.

"I think," she said with dignity, "that I should go into the pa-hay-okee, the Everglades, where these spirits dwell, and stay until I hear the animals talk, see the serpent and meet the little people who live underground."

She waited for Charlie Wind to shake his head "no."

"Good," he said, much to her surprise. Promptly he turned to Mary Wind, who was two years older than she.

"Mary Wind," he said to the sturdy fifteen-year-old, who had been the one to tell the medicine man about Billie Wind's doubts, "go with your sister in the tribal dugout as far as Lost Dog Island. There you will find an ancient dugout pulled up on the alligator beach. In it are three white heron feathers. Wave them over Billie Wind so that she will have a safe journey. Then come on home."

Crossing his feet, he sat down among the councilmen, who were meeting, as they did once a year, on the tribal island of Panther Paw in the Everglades to settle arguments and reprimand the offenders of the Seminole laws. The Big Cypress Reservation, where they farmed and raised cattle, was about thirty miles west of their island. Most of the clan would return to their farms and homes after the four-day Green Corn Dance festival that would start the day after tomorrow.

Billie Wind was well known for her curiosity. Only last summer she had peeked through the cane screen at the rear of the council house to watch Charlie Wind open the sacred medicine bundle. Her foot had slipped, and she had knocked the screen over.

"What are you doing?" he had asked in surprise.

"Trying to see the magic in the medicine bundle," she had answered. "I want to see what makes the rain fall and cures the sick."

"And what did you see?"

"Nothing," she had answered honestly. "Just some minerals and stones, a snake's fang and the flint and steel you start the Green Corn Dance fires with—also some herbs." She had tipped her head inquiringly. "Do they *really* make the rain fall and cure the sick?"

Charlie Wind had not answered immediately. Instead he had reached for a feather broom, swept the ground, sat down and gestured for her to sit beside him.

"The medicine bundle," he had said, leaning so close that she could see the dust in the wrinkles of his face, "was given to two ancient medicine men by the adopted son of the Corn Mother.

"The bundle was divided between them, and they divided their bundles into forty more—one for each clan. When the Spaniards came to Florida they killed and ravaged and warred upon the ancient people. Most of the medicine bundles were burned or lost. Some were hidden and never have been found again. Only eight still exist. And this is one of them." He reverently patted the leather pouch with his long fingers. "And that makes it magical to me."

"But it doesn't really make the rain fall, does it, Charlie Wind?"

"Yes," he had answered.

"But you have asked the sky to rain every day for a year and it hasn't rained. South Florida is still dry. Our gardens are shriveling."

"You are too practical," he said. "That is the white man's trait. There is more to the Earth than only the things you can see with your eyes."

"What are they?" she asked with great sincerity. "I would love to see what isn't there."

"You are a doubter." He shook his head; then, holding his hands, palms up, to the sky, he closed his eyes.

Presently he opened them.

"I will teach you how to see something that is not there," he had said. "You must find two lightning bolts and bring them to me."

"Two lightning bolts?" she said with astonishment. "I can't do that."

"You must. Then you will see. Now, go along and find them." He dismissed her with the back of his hand.

Billie Wind walked out of the council house and leaned against the trunk of an avocado tree. A mourning dove cooed to her large babies, who were balanced on a limb above Billie. Billie Wind studied them as if the answer to this odd assignment would come from the lovely birds. No answer. Perhaps an inspiration would come from her grandmother in the communal kitchen, who was bent over the fire stirring a pot with one hand while holding her full, bright, yellow-and-red skirt with the other. None came. She glanced at her family's chickee, an open home with a platform for sleeping and a roof thatched with palm leaves. Her mother, Whispering Wind, was at the sewing machine, pumping it with her foot and putting together small pieces of bright cotton. She saw no lightning bolts there; just Whispering Wind's warm silhouette against the sunny sky.

She wondered how her mother would solve this problem. Whispering Wind would think of something; for, like Billie, she was very practical. She had to be. She was the head of the Wind Clan and dealt with many problems that the medicine man and the councilmen did not: settling arguments, encouraging leadership and giving self-confidence.

"Lightning bolts," Billie Wind mumbled. "Where? Where?"

On the far side of the open common another uncle was stirring the ceremonial cauldron as he brewed red willow, lizard's-tail plants and ginseng. He sang as he mixed the "black drink," a special brew that is made once a year for the Green Corn Dance. She smiled. The black drink was a lightning bolt if ever there was one. When the councilmen drank it on the second day of the festival they danced like tornadoes and threw spears higher than rockets could soar. They saw demons and future events, then fell as if struck by lightning.

"I'll bring Charlie Wind two cups of the black drink," she said mischievously, then became serious. "Where am I going to find two lightning bolts? Does Charlie Wind want me to say I can not find any? What does he want? Lightning strikes and is gone. It leaps from cloud to cloud, and cloud to ground. It does not stay still. I can not catch it.

"And Charlie Wind knows that. So what does he want of me?"

"Billie Wind," her mother called. "Come to the chickee. You must finish stitching your dancing shoes for the festival." Mamau Whispering Wind was seated cross-legged on the table-high platform in the chickee. Beside her lay pillows, pots, dishes, a radio, canned foods, blankets and a sewing machine. The earthen floor of the chickee had been swept clean for the day.

"I can't right now," Billie Wind said. "I have to perform a miracle for Charlie Wind." She sighed and her mother's eyes softened kindly as if to say: "So he's up to miracles again."

The shoes Billie Wind was making were for the dances that celebrated the ripening of the corn crop the Seminoles grew in their gardens. The festival was only one day away, and she had hours of work before her. She must also make a turban for her brother. This year he had been chosen to go into the pa-hay-okee to kill and bring home a white heron. The feathers would be hung from the poles that would be carried in the Feather Dance. She should not be wasting time looking for lightning bolts that could not be found. She should be getting ready for the day after tomorrow, a hallowed day in late June.

On that day the men and boys would clean the dancing ground, repair chickees and take ceremonial baths. They would gather wood, and Charlie Wind would light the fire after sundown. There would be dancing and games. On the next day the men would feast in the council house, then join the rest of the tribe with more dancing and game playing.

On the third day the medicine man would bathe and bring out the sacred medicine bundle. Charlie Wind would open it before the councilmen and they would pass judgment on those who had disobeyed the tribal laws. They would then toss the first corn of the year into the black drink and drink it at midnight. The Feather Dance, the Woodpecker Dance and the Buffalo Dance would be performed until the sun came up. Billie Wind would dance with the women. On the dawn of the fourth day the sacred bundle would be hidden for another year, and when that was done the entire tribe would feast on the new corn. They would dance in celebration of all the forces that had made the harvest a success: the sun, the rain, the darkness of night and all the animals that they had seen during the good season.

With all this excitement to prepare for, Billie Wind was annoyed that she had to find two lightning bolts. She kicked a stone and wondered what to do. She would turn around in a complete circle, and if no idea came, she would give up.

Halfway around she saw two spider lilies far out in the saw grass. Their long white petals folded back from thin golden centers like the sparks of a lightning bolt. She rolled up her blue jeans, waded out through the shallow glades to the lilies and with a flick of her penknife cut off the flowers. Then she splashed back to Panther Paw Island.

"Here are the lightning bolts," she had said to Charlie Wind, her eyes shining with the fun of her joke. She waited for him to send her out for real lightning bolts. He did not.

"Yes," he said, looking closely at the flowers. "They are indeed."

Billie Wind stared at the medicine man as if to see

the circuits and cells inside his head that made him think so strangely.

"Yes," he repeated. "These *are* lightning bolts." And for a flash of a moment Billie Wind almost understood something profound; but not quite.

That had been a year ago. And now, here she was again, led into trouble by her curiosity.

"The tribal dugout will be waiting for you at the airboat dock tomorrow morning at sunup," Charlie Wind said. "Stay one night and two days and come home."

She walked out of the council house, wondering why she had imposed such a punishment on herself. She wanted to dance and play games. Why hadn't she suggested she sweep the dancing ground? The councilmen would have accepted that as punishment. But no, she was so stubborn and curious she had to suggest a crazy long voyage. She walked home and sat in the shadow of the chickee, feeling sorry for herself.

The next morning she was cheered by the rising sun. It shone like a red penny through the mist. She woke Mary, and they walked through the silvery dew to the dugout. It was tied beside the airboat, a flat boat with a motorized fan that "blew" passengers across the saw grass in the watery prairie the Indians called the pa-hay-okee. She looked at the airboat, which carried the children to the Indian school on Big Cypress Reservation and the men to islands to hunt and fish. Then she looked at the dugout, a beautiful, simple craft chopped and burned from a cypress tree by Charlie Wind himself.

"Sit in the bow," she said to Mary, who wore her traditional Seminole cape for the occasion, an airy circle of cloth with a hole in the center for her head. It fell gracefully over her shoulders to her waist. Below she wore a skirt of brilliantly colored patchwork, the hallmark of the Seminole Indians. The skirt was made of tiny patches, one inch square and smaller, sewn together to form intricate designs. Mary's was a blue, green, yellow and black mosaic and was startlingly beautiful. Billie Wind looked at her sister.

"Why did you tell Charlie Wind on me?"

"Because you are too scientific. You are realistic like the white men."

"I see what I see. What I don't see, I don't believe."

"You were not that way before you went to the school at the Kennedy Space Center when our father worked for the scientists."

"That's not true. I've always been curious. I want answers, not legends. What is the matter with that?"

"What is the matter with that? I'll tell you. Someday you will be the head of your family and you'll need to know more than facts."

Billie Wind did not answer her. Lost Dog Island was just ahead; she would be glad to be rid of Mary and alone in the glades. The sun was up, the frogs had quieted down and the birds were calling to each other as they awoke and assembled for the day. She could take just so much of her sister and all her righteousness. She poled swiftly.

Billie Wind was tall for her age. Her frame was lithe like a reed, a gift from her Calusa ancestors who had lived in the Everglades for unknown thousands of years before the Spanish conquistadores arrived in the late 1550s. Her high cheekbones were reminiscent of her Hitchiti ancestors, members of the Creek Confederacy who were driven out of Georgia by the Colonial Army around 1750. The Creeks had joined forces with escaped Black slaves and, as one clan, they had crossed Lake Okeechobee and vanished into what the white men called, at that time, the unholy swamp. Here they had lived well on the abundant game, fruits and succulent plants. Isolated in the wilderness they had become proud and independent and had established governments to help them live in balance with the land. They had never signed a peace treaty with the U.S. government. Even today they are at war with the United States. The white men called these strong, intelligent people the Sem-in-oli, meaning "wild" in the Hitchiti language.

Billie Wind was approaching Lost Dog Island on a hundred-year-old alligator trail, a trail swept free of grass and plants by the heavy reptiles dragging tails and bodies from one island or pool to the next. She watched for alligators as she poled. A big one, ten to twelve feet long, could upset a dugout with one whack of its tail. She saw only one small gator. As she approached the island she leaned on her pole and sent the boat flying up onto the beach.

"I see the dugout," Mary said brightly and, checking

the beach for alligators, stepped ashore. She quickly found the feathers and turned around just as Billie Wind gave her boat a shove and slid out into the water.

"Billie Wind. Come back!" Mary shouted. "Charlie Wind told me . . ."

"I don't want any silly feathers waved over my boat," she answered, poling into the deep water at the end of the island.

"Billie Wind." Mary's voice broke into many voices as it bounced off the thousands of three-sided saw grass blades nourished by the shallow waters of the glades. When the sound finally reached Billie's ear it was more like a lost ibis crying than her sister. She rounded the island and poled until she could not hear Mary anymore, then she stopped and looked at the glittering Everglades, the river of grass, the unholy swamp, the pa-hay-okee.

Each saw grass blade glistened like a copper spear in the hot June sun. Many hundreds of white birds skimmed over the swamp water. Their reflections skimmed under them. In the distance, gray-green islands like Panther Paw resembled ships sailing against the brilliant blue sky. The Everglades was flat and as luminous as winter's southern seas.

And that was all she saw—grass-filled water, birds, sky and islands like her own. She was in an immense wilderness larger than the state of Delaware, and as glorious as birds in flight.

She felt comforted. Her hurt was gone. The water sparkled, the sky shone sea blue. She would stay out here all day and go home tomorrow. "And what will I tell Charlie Wind? I know. I will say I saw the serpent, heard talking animals and danced with the little people." She listened to the stiff saw grass scratch the side of her boat. "If he thinks a lily is a lightning bolt, then I will tell him the wind is an animal god who talks." She thought better of that.

"No, I'm not going to lie. I'll stay here until I hear and see something . . . even"—she felt the tears rising—"even if I have to miss all of the Green Corn Dance festival."

By midmorning she had poled out of the saw grass and into Lost Dog Slough. This was a natural channel, a river within a river. Here the water flowed a bit more swiftly. The saw grass could not grow in it for the water ran deep. Even her pole would not touch bottom. She picked up the paddle and gently moved the boat along.

Water lilies bloomed pertly at the edges of the slough and underwater plants made forests below the surface. Billie Wind leaned over the side of the boat and watched schools of two-inch mosquito fish swim along trails in the submerged forests. One little fish swallowed a mosquito larva that was wriggling toward the surface for air. A long-nosed garfish swallowed the mosquito fish.

"And who will eat you?" she asked the garfish.

"Bulldozers, canal diggers and nuclear bombs," she answered, quoting her father and her teacher at the Kennedy Space Center School. "Then people will move to another planet, a planet that the spaceships will find circling another sun. Five-course dinners will grow on trees and there will be beds of orchids to sleep on. Medicine men will be scientists and children will be born knowing everything." She dreamed of the faraway planet and poled on into the wilderness.

When she could no longer see Lost Dog Island on the flat horizon she leaned back to rest. Her shoulders struck something hard. Putting down the paddle she reached back and pulled out a deerskin pouch that had been tucked into the tip of the stern. It belonged to her mother, Mamau Whispering Wind. Billie Wind smiled to see it, for Mamau like herself was realistic. Charlie Wind would wave white heron feathers over her boat for good luck, but her mother would give her tools and food to make certain her journey was safe.

The pouch contained two generous pieces of smoked venison, a loaf of corn bread, coconut meat, a machete for cutting down brush and a magnifying glass with which to start fires. Under the machete she found one of the string hammocks Whispering Wind could make so well, and beneath it her own sneakers and leather leggings. She would need them if she had to walk any distance in the cutting saw grass.

"Mamau Whispering Wind is a good thinker. She knows I could get lost or have an accident out here, so she's taken precautions." As she checked her hip pocket for her penknife, she saw that a fish spear had been tucked under the seat in the bow of the dugout.

"Dear Mamau Whispering Wind," she said. "You are my three white heron feathers."

She picked up the paddle again, dipped it into the smooth water and paddled on and on down the glistening pa-hay-okee.

The Serpent

 The dugout slipped over the surface, riding high and quietly like a leaf. The breeze died down, the air warmed toward ninety degrees Fahrenheit, and the heat became an ominous presence that stifled even the movements of the birds. They stopped feeding and sought the shade of the distant tree islands. On the other hand, the mosquito wrigglers changed into winged adults in the glorious heat and arose from the surface of the water like smoke. Instantly they were pursued by squadrons of bomber-shaped dragonflies, who gobbled them up.

The snakes liked the hot temperature. They slithered

through the water, hunting delicacies. They moved swiftly, one after another, on both sides of the boat, their pointed heads above water, making ripples.

"There are an awful lot of snakes out here," Billie Wind finally said to herself. "And they all seem to be moving west to east across Lost Dog Slough. And that's strange."

And the alligators were restless. On other trips down the slough, she had seen them hang quietly at the surface, eyes jutting above the water, watching and waiting for food. Today they were zigzagging beneath the surface of the water. She did not know why. Probably because it was hot, so hot in fact that she finally pulled her black hair over her face to make shade and stopped exerting herself. She lay back in the dugout and let the current carry her.

She drifted only a few feet a minute, for the water of the Everglades creeps. It is a slow river. Once, it seeped out of Lake Okeechobee, before canals were dug to drain the land south of the lake for farming. Now the river comes from rainfall only. It is one hundred miles long and seventy-five miles wide and ends in Florida Bay.

Drifting down the river of grass, Billie Wind could see the sun and the water and soils at work. Flowers bloomed before her eyes. Butterflies drank the nectar of the flowers and red-winged blackbirds ate the butterflies. The snakes ate the blackbirds and the alligators ate the snakes. Charlie Wind was right, all life came from the sun and the water and the soil and the air.

Just before noon the first clouds of the day formed on the horizon. They were small, the size of sheep. Billie Wind watched them gather and grow into mountainous billows that cast shadows on the saw grass, turning it from copper green to purple-brown.

A large mud turtle surfaced near her boat, took a breath and submerged. He swam laboriously toward the east with the snakes and alligators.

"See, Charlie Wind," she said. "Here beside me is the spirit of the turtle. He is beautiful but he does not speak."

A large-mouthed bass came close to the surface and paused. Grasping her spear she stood over him, thrust and missed. The spear shot down into the water and then popped up, for the stem was bamboo, and its joints were filled with air. She scooped up the spear and practiced on a floating leaf. Spearing fish was not as easy as her father made it appear to be.

The sounds of the glades were strange this day. Squawks, screams, croaks and pipings floated across the humid air. As she listened and dozed, her mind wandered back to the Space Center, where she and her brother had spent two winters with their father, Iron Wind. Mary had chosen not to go to school at the Space Center while Iron Wind worked on the launcher for the Voyager spaceships that explored the planets. So she did not know about astronomy and the quest for life in space. She knew only of serpents and talking animal gods and dwarfs.

And Mary had not heard Iron Wind when he said to

Billie one evening in their trailer home: "We may need to move off the Earth someday. We are polluting this planet with chemicals and radiation from atomic weapons and nuclear reactors. Mankind is forcing mankind out into space to find another planet."

When Iron Wind worked at night Billie would wait for him outside the Space Life lab, staring up at the stars and wondering which one had a sapphire-blue planet with an Everglades and a girl like herself looking out toward her.

The dugout bumped into a clump of alligator flags, tall plants with single leaves growing like flags atop the bare stems. The plants got their name from these leaves and the fact that they usually surrounded alligator pools. Taking heed of this, she paddled around the plants into a clump of willows, drifted past the willows and came upon an alligator trail she had never seen before. She stood up to better see where it led. The trail wound for miles across the glittery pa-hay-okee to a green island. The island's dark color told her that it was a "hardwood hammock," not an island of willows or even of cypress trees like Lost Dog Island, but an island that grew mahogany and gumbo-limbo trees. There would be live oaks and bustic trees on the hammock as well as royal palms and pond apples. It was a wild island—unlike Panther Paw, which was planted to oranges, coconuts, papayas and corn. The limestone on the island would be pitted with sinkholes, deep wells leached by the acids from the plants. Orchids and ferns would festoon the trees and the floor of the forest, and its glades would be damp and cool.

"That's where I will spend the night," she said. "If any animal is going to talk, he'll talk to me there on that wild, natural island."

Billie Wind poled along the alligator trail. It wound and twisted through the reeds, crossed sloughs, then bee-lined through the saw grass for many miles.

The white clouds became purple thunderheads. They roiled and flashed with lightning. For the first time in almost two years she hoped they would not pour down rain although the glades needed it. The water was so low in places that the mud of lime and plant cells, called marl, was cracked and dry, and the saw grass that grew in it was withered. The only water in many places was in the alligator holes and trails, and some of these had now gone dry. Not far from Panther Paw a gator hole had dried up, sending the great reptiles down into the marl to estivate, to go into a protective sleep as some animals do in hot, dry weather.

She poled into an area where there were only a few feet of water in the deeply cut alligator trail. The boat stopped. She walked to the bow, put her pole in the marl, hung on to it, kicked the boat forward and dropped back into the stern. In this manner she moved slowly across the blazing glades.

A thunderhead flashed with lightning. She looked up.

"Are you going to rain?" she asked the clouds by way of testing the voice of the thunderbird god. "Answer me!" A clap of thunder banged overhead with such force that she jumped. "I'm sorry. I'm sorry," she called. "I believe you are there. I believe you are there." Then she grinned.

About a hundred yards from the island she stopped poling and blinked both eyes. The island had disappeared. Was the swamp playing mysterious tricks on her? She shivered and stood up. The island returned to view six feet above the horizon line.

"Mirage," she said taking up the pole again, but she was unconvinced. The heat was not dry enough for a mirage. She moved forward gingerly, then a cloud passed over the sun and the island dropped to its proper place.

"If I didn't know better, I would say it was Charlie Wind scaring me with magic from the snake fang."

The island rose again, and although she knew there was some reasonable answer for the phenomenon she could not fathom it. A hot wind blew against her face. She gasped, for it was so intensely hot that she expected to see a rocket low overhead. Nothing was to be seen.

The wind changed; a cooler breeze nudged her face, and she headed for a small beach under a cabbage palm.

Out of the water rose a tail so large it could have belonged to a whale. It was sheathed in heavy armor and spiked with sharp ridges. The monstrous tail came straight toward her. She dropped to the bottom of the dugout as a mammoth alligator struck the stern of the boat and catapulted it forward. It rocked, tipped, but not quite over, then hit the beach with a crack. Billie Wind jumped ashore as a fifteen-foot alligator slammed his jaws closed on the rear of the boat. The wood splintered.

"Yo! yo!" She jabbed her pole at the monster. He grunted, spat out the wood and sank beneath the surface of the water.

A boiling turbulence marked his flight to the bottom of the moat that surrounded the island. The moat was maintained by the alligators who weeded and dug it deep with their mouths and tails. They pushed the debris ashore, leaving the water sparkling and clear. For their efforts the fish and turtles multiplied, and they ate their abundant crop.

Shaking from the scare, she pulled the dugout up on the shore, saw that the damage was slight and tied it to the cabbage palm. She threw her deerskin pouch over her shoulder, pushed back the limbs of a shrub and stepped into a hauntingly beautiful forest.

Gwad! someone screamed.

HO, HO, HO, HOHO.

Crank.

Billie Wind cast her eyes around the dim forest. Tree trunks were gnarled totems. Their limbs were draped with shrouds of Spanish moss. Some were homes to air plants and ferns.

Gwad. The screamer flashed through the trees and Billie Wind let out her breath.

"Woodpecker."

Crank.

"Wood ibis." She liked playing the game and laughed.

"They do sound like people," she mused to herself. "I guess that's what Charlie Wind means when he says that the animal gods talk.

"But that isn't talk; not really."

Git! Git! Git!

"Or is it? Is that crazy anhinga, that snake-necked water bird, telling me to get out of here?" She walked slowly.

"There is something strange here. The air? the silence? the deadly smell?"

A few feet into the forest she came upon a cocoplum bush laden with plumlike fruits. She paused and popped the tart fruits into her mouth, then wended her way through a valley of ten-foot-high conte ferns and found herself in a mossy glade. Its odor was fresh with the smell of growing things. Nearby an enormous strangler fig dropped cascades of roots from its limbs, forming corridors and caverns.

Ho!

"*Ho,* yourself, Chief Barred Owl," she called, pleased to know what he was.

"If that is talk, then I'm an owl, too. *HO, HO, HOHOHO!*" Presently a dark form came toward her through the gloom. The owl was approaching on flight feathers that made no sound. He swept up to a limb directly above her and folded his soft wings to his body. He swung his head from side to side, trying to identify the owl that he had heard. He bobbed his head up and down to better hear her sounds.

"Hello," she said. "I am a person. You came because you thought I was an owl.

"I can hoot your language, but you can not speak mine."

She crossed the glade to a cluster of strap ferns with their long thin leaves, pushed past them and came upon a circle of soft lichens and moss. She swung her pouch to the ground.

"This is my magic spot. I will sleep here and listen to the animals talk."

She selected two trees about six feet apart, from which she would sling her hammock, and was pulling it from her pack when she heard a strange wind.

She stood up. It whined like something alive.

"But it isn't a bird or a beast." Curious, she wended her way among vines and figs, across the island toward the sound. Pushing back the shoreline bushes she looked out on the endless expanse of saw grass prairie. There was no water gleaming in it. The blades were brown and dead. Gray clouds rolled and billowed.

"Rain," she cheered. "It really *is* going to rain. These clouds are not teasing." As she ran back to gather up her possessions she kept an eye out for a shelter. A deep sinkhole that looked like an open well caught her attention. It was almost fifteen feet deep and wide "and probably has caves in it, as most sinkholes do," she said as she let herself down a few feet to a ledge in the pit.

Below she saw her reflection in a pool.

"Water. That's good. Water erodes caves." Another ledge lay below the first and she dropped to that. From there it was an easy scramble to the bottom of the pit, where a huge log lay half submerged in the pool. She stepped upon it, bent down and peered into a cave.

"Lucky me," she said aloud. "See there, Charlie Wind, I didn't need three white heron feathers." She leaped from the log into the cave. The sandy floor was pocked with the inverted funnels of ant lions. The little insects sit at the bottom of these funnels that are really traps, waiting for traveling ants to slip and slide down. The pits are pitched at such a steep angle the ants can not climb out. They fall prey to the little killers.

"The ant lions tell me something," she said. "They build pits only in dry places; so this cave is dry. That's good."

She returned to her possessions and, slinging the pouch over her shoulder, hurried toward the pit. A deer, ears back, eyes wide with fright, bolted across the mound and ran full speed for the far side of the island where her dugout was beached.

"What's the matter with you?" she called to the deer. "Is the storm that bad?" The deer was silent. "Please talk," she called facetiously.

A marsh rabbit bounded over the ferns, running full out for the far side of the island. He zigged and zagged as rabbits do to confuse an enemy.

The barred owl took off toward the east, and overhead, a flock of wood storks frantically winged in the same direction. They squawked as they kept in touch with each other.

"What's going on?" she called to them. "Let Charlie Wind be right. Speak. Tell me why all the animals are frightened."

Hardly had she spoken than she was struck by a blast of hot air, more searing than the one she had felt in the boat. It smelled of burning grass. And then she knew; she knew why the animals ran and why the island seemed to rise.

"Fire," she gasped. "This is no thunderstorm. The prairie is burning."

Now she could see flames through the trees. Running to the shore, she pushed back the limbs and looked out. Orange blazes licked the sky like serpents' tongues. They shot downward and devoured the grass. They spat black smoke as the many-tongued beast came rushing toward Billie Wind.

"The boat!" She turned and ran. Near the pit she thought better of escaping in the dugout. "I can't paddle hard enough. The fire is coming too fast."

The cave was her only hope. Letting herself over the edge of the sinkhole, she clambered down to the log, jumped into the water to wet herself down so she would not burn, and ran into the cave. She looked up.

Yellow and red fireballs shot through the trees. A live oak burst into flame; a mahogany tree shimmered in the heat, then exploded in fire. Billie Wind had seen all she wanted to see. Creeping deep into the cave, she hugged her calves and dropped her head onto her knees.

After a long while she looked up. The island was a fire box. Green limbs came to a boil and exploded like bullets. Flames ran up and around the trees like slithering serpents: millions and millions of them. A burning limb fell into the pit, struck the water, hissed like a snake and went out.

A deer screamed.

Fires in the Everglades are necessary. Billie Wind knew this. They burned seedling trees out of the pa-hay-okee so that only grass would grow. They thinned out the underbrush on the islands, and because the fires were frequent, they never became hot enough to burn the island trees. Hardwood hammocks like the one Billie Wind was on were protected by moisture from the plants, and they rarely if ever burned. The fires were simply not hot enough to penetrate them. And this had gone on for twenty thousand years. Then the practical white man fought and put out the Everglades fires. The underbrush grew dense and thick. Now, when fires start in the glades they burn hot, and they sweep through the islands, killing the trees and burning down into the rich humus.

The fire that roared above Billie Wind glowed like a blast furnace. It created rising winds that carried sticks and limbs high into the sky.

Inside the cave Billie Wind watched uneasily as flaming limbs dropped from the smoke clouds into the pit. A turtle plunged off the rim and splashed into the water. Lizards dropped like rain from the hot trees, and an armadillo, North America's relative of the sloth, crept to a ledge. His armoured back was singed and sooty. He lifted his head, slipped and fell ten feet into the water. He did not come up.

Snakes slithered down the wall of the pit. Billie Wind counted more than a dozen before she lowered her eyes and curled up in a ball to sleep. She could not.

She wondered if her tribe could see the fire, and if so, would they try to rescue her?

"They won't," she remembered sadly. "I was curious once too often. Mary will tell them I went south down Lost Dog Slough instead of west. They will not look for me. They will think I am safe. Fires burn as the wind blows. This wind is from west to east."

She lay very still watching the reflected flames dance in the water and listening to the crackle and roar of the fire.

"Charlie Wind," she said after a long while, "there *is* a serpent."

An hour before dawn, Billie Wind, who had not slept all night, lifted her head and looked up at the fire. It still raged. She pushed farther back in the cave. As she moved, her hand struck something hard and round. She brought it close to her face for inspection. It was a clay bowl.

"Burial ground," she said. "This is a burial ground of the Seminoles. I should not be here." Nervously she went to the entrance and held the bowl in the light of the fire shining down from above. Around its rim were feathery drawings. Her fingers ran lightly over the coils of clay that formed the dark bowl. It was gritty to her touch. The grittiness was typical of bowls fired in sand by the ancient Indians.

"Calusa," she said. "This is a Calusa pot." She glanced around the cave. "This place is very old; very, very old. The Calusas were killed off four hundred years ago.

"And it is not a burial ground. Burial pots are broken to let the spirits out.

"Someone lived here. Some ancient ancestor lived in this cave." The light flared up and she crawled around the room on hands and knees curious to see and learn. Near the far wall she found a conch shell. A hole had been drilled through it, and the tough, thick lip had been ground to a sharp edge.

"A pick," she said. "Hey, ghostly ancestor, you had a pick. Who were you and why were you down here in this cave?" She rocked back on her heels and saw that there was a long niche chipped into the wall.

"A bed." She climbed into it, stretched out and discovered that her head and feet touched the walls. "The ancestor was not much taller than I," she observed; then a thought occurred to her. She felt for human bones. To her relief she found none. "You did not die here," she said aloud. "You lived, and so will I."

As the sun came up the mood of the fire changed. The crackle and roar became a soft hum. The mist of morning was drifting across the island and seeping down into the pit. The air smelled of smoke and tree resin. Billie Wind coughed, took off her shirt and dipped it in the water. She held it over her nose and mouth to filter out the smoke. Lying on her belly, facedown, she breathed the heavy, cold air that still lay along the floor of the cave.

As the morning waned, the smoky mist vanished, leaving the air almost fresh. Billie Wind removed her filter, sat up and breathed deeply. A new sound was on the wind. It was a hiss, and beyond the hiss a splat.

"Rain!" she cried. "Mamau Whispering Wind, I hear rain. I'm all right. I'm all right."

Taking off her leggings and sneakers, clutching the bowl to her chest, she climbed into the bed of the ancient person and lay down. She closed her eyes and this time she did sleep.

Petang

 Billie Wind awoke around noon but she did not get up. Instead she lay quietly on her back, staring at the limestone wall. Where was she? Why was she looking at a wall? With a shiver she remembered. She was entombed by the fire serpent. She felt her legs. "I'm alive." Then she added, "I think." She moved her fingers and toes. "Yes, I am." Turning cautiously to her side, she peered out of the cave. The roaring fire of last night could not be heard. She sat up. The sun fell in pale patches on the log and the pool. The air was smoky but sunlit.

Sliding from her bed she walked out on the log and

looked up. A few strands of smoke curled along the rim of the pit; an occasional flare marked the last gasp of a flame. The trees were black stalks, and the once lacy green canopy was gone. Although hot coals glowed along the rim of the pit, the worst of the fire seemed to be over. She was cheered. As her shoulders relaxed she became aware of a gnawing hunger and took out Mamau Whispering Wind's corn bread. She ate all but a small bite, then squatted on her heels and studied the sinkhole and sky. Where the walls had been festooned with ferns and mosses yesterday, they were now bare. Without the plants as a cover, she could see that there were not just two ledges in the pit, but many. She studied them.

"Steps," she said. "I think they are steps. And steps are cut by persons." She crossed the log and measured them with her hand. "Yes, they are. Some person came and went on them." She pondered as to who it might have been. "Perhaps she was hiding from a fire . . . like me. No, fires did not burn the moist islands in those days. Perhaps she hid from the conquistadores. Or maybe she was the leader of the little underground people, and this was the stairway to her council house." She smiled at her joke. "I wish it were so—then I could go home and tell Charlie Wind there *are* little underground people who build strange cities and save curious little Seminole Indian girls."

She pushed the little people out of her head and considered the stairs again. They were pocked and black with fire burn and oxidation; old but maybe not ancient. The

Calusa built ramps. White men and Seminoles built steps. And yet, the Everglades and the south Florida west coast were dotted with the ruins of many ingenious constructions; canals that led to fish-holding ponds, elevated village sites. One such structure lay just south of Big Cypress Reservation. Billie Wind and her mother had found shards of pottery there, black and rough like her pot.

"Where did the ancient people come from?" she had asked Whispering Wind as she turned a piece over in her hands.

"From Asia," she had answered. "They crossed the Bering land bridge to North America thousands and thousands of years ago with all the other American Indians. And they moved southward for thousands of years until they found the beautiful pa-hay-okee and lived in health and peace. The Great Spirit was good to them and to Florida."

Iron Wind told her this when she asked him:

"Some men say that the Calusa came across the Gulf of Mexico from Yucatan, because Calusa mounds resembled the Mayan mounds. I don't think so. But no one knows for sure, and unless we find new clues in the ruins, we'll never know."

She had pondered enough. She jumped down the steps to pack up her possessions and leave. She was eager to go home.

The bowl she packed carefully, wrapping it many times in the hammock. She would show it to Charlie Wind and he would send historical detectives to the island.

She pulled on her sneakers and leggings, checked her pocket to make sure her penknife was there, shouldered her pouch and ran across the log and up the steps. Near the top she was stopped by a blast of heat. She covered her face with her arm. The stones and soil were oven hot. She could not touch anything. Standing on her tiptoes, she peered over the rim of the pit. Flames leaped along fallen trees and red fires smouldered in the loam.

"I'm trapped," she said. "The earth is too hot to walk on." Biting her lips to keep them from trembling she turned and walked slowly back to the cave.

"I can't wait very long," she said. "I've got one piece of venison left." She sat down on the bed. "I'm going to die here. It will take a long, long time for the earth to cool. I shall die in this pit." She dropped her head on her knees.

Presently a thought replaced her fear. She remembered that a tortoise had fallen into the water and that many, many snakes had slithered into the pit. All were good food. She unpacked her deerskin pouch, placed the pot on the ground and pondered.

In the light of the afternoon she saw that the bumps on the floor of the cave that she had thought to be rocks last night were piles of oysters, conches and cochinas. The sea must have been a short distance away when the ancient person lived here. Charlie Wind told old legends about the sea once covering all the pa-hay-okee. Maybe he was right.

Taking out her machete, she dug into a shell pile and

uncovered a conch with its top cut off and the inside spiral removed.

"A cup," she exclaimed, recognizing the object from ones like it at Panther Paw. She put the cup aside and dug more carefully into the broken shells and dust. A few inches down she uncovered an oyster shell that had been chipped into a stirring spoon and near it, the heavy central column of an enormous fighting conch.

"A hammer." She brought it down sharply on the ground, and was surprised by how well it was balanced. She dug on, uncovering a wedge-shaped conch with a sharp edge. Two holes had been drilled in this instrument, which she recognized to be an adz.

"Like the steel one Charlie Wind uses to hew dugouts," she said and planned a new handle for it by running a rope from her hammock through the two holes and knotting it around a stick. The shell, though old, was still strong. She put it aside. After uncovering a few more cups and spoons, broken and unbroken, she noticed that the far wall was blackened.

"A cooking hearth," she said, wondering where the smoke vented. She glanced up and saw that the roof of the cave was riddled with holes typical of the Everglades limestone. The smoke, of course, went up through the porous rock.

A shrill whistle sounded. Billie Wind leaped to her feet and ran joyfully to the entrance of the cave.

"Charlie Wind!" she cried, recognizing his call to council. "I'm here. I'm here." She crossed the log and climbed up the stairs.

"Hello, Charlie Wind!" She slowed as she neared the top. It couldn't be Charlie Wind. The earth was a red-hot inferno. Not even a medicine man could cross it. She peered at the smouldering forest floor.

No one was there.

Her hopes shattered, she sat down on a step and covered her face with her hands. She felt alone and frightened, even more so than that moment when she saw the fire coming toward her.

The whistle sounded again.

She lifted her head with renewed interest. "It's coming from inside the wall of the pit."

Someone grunted and coughed in a sooty hole at her feet. She leaned over and peered into a shadowy cavern.

"Who's there?" The humanlike cough sounded again. Two bright eyes gleamed above a flat nose and upturned mouth. "I see a little person," she said, then added aloud: "Charlie Wind, forgive me." She thought again. This time more clearly. "Nonsense, there are no such things as little underground men."

The mouth in the hole moved as if to speak and she saw that the lips were rimmed with silvery whiskers.

"A petang, a petang," she cried joyfully. "Little otter, what are you doing here?" Holding out her hand she waited for him to smell her odor of friendship and come to her. Last year a black bear on Panther Paw had smelled her affection and had walked almost up to her before turning away.

But this little animal did not move. He huddled in the darkness. He was badly frightened. After a long wait Billie Wind tiptoed down the steps and brought back the last piece of venison, which she chewed to soften. The petang twirled his whiskers and sniffed the food.

"Come, little friend," she said. "Come here to me. I shall take care of you whom the Indians of the north call petang.

"We are the only living things in this whole charred and black world."

Petang's nostrils flared. He backed up.

"Did you escape the fire by crawling into a pit like me? If so, we are fire spirits. We must console each other." Petang's eyes rolled from right to left and then up into Billie Wind's face. He seemed to sense something reassuring about her, for he poked his head out of the hole and whimpered. Then he grabbed the meat in his small teeth so vigorously that Billie Wind was forced to hold it with both hands.

"You are very strong," she said. "And very young," she added, for he stopped pulling and began sucking. "You are still nursing." She peered behind him into the hole to see if the mother otter was hiding there. She was not.

Hesitatingly, moving forward, back, forward, the little otter finally came all the way out of the hole and, placing one large, webbed foot on her hand, grunted wistfully.

Then he sat up, propping himself erect like a little man with the support of his stout, tapering tail. Strong muscles rippled under his silver-brown fur. Billie Wind judged him to be about two months old, for she had once played with a young otter at the zoo on the Big Cypress Reservation. This little fellow was about the size of a marsh rabbit. He would grow to be about three feet long and nine or ten inches high at the shoulder.

Talking softly to this beautiful friend, she slipped one hand under him and drew him to her with the other. She held him against her body, stroking his head and body as do mother otters to encourage their little ones to eat. He sucked the meat. At the same time she peered into other holes searching for a mother or sister or brother. She saw nothing else alive, not even a snake, not even a mosquito. Then a frog piped from the bottom of the sinkhole.

"That makes three of us," she said. "You and me, Petang, and a frog."

Petang devoured most of the venison by simply sucking it down. When he was satisfied, he snuggled against her and instantly fell asleep. She was happy to see him relax, for it meant that he trusted her. Gingerly tiptoeing, so as not to awaken him, she carried the little otter to the cave and sat down. She wondered what to do next. She must hunt food, and yet she did not want to put him down for fear he would run away.

She stroked his head. He snuggled closer making the soft grunts and snorts little otters make to their mothers.

Billie Wind was encouraged, for the noises said to her that the petang was accepting her as a substitute mother. He might stay with her. She had fed and stroked him, and that, she knew, spelled "mother" to all young mammals. Presently he folded his paws on his chest as if to say his world was all right again. Like the other members of his lively family, the mink, the weasel, the skunk and the wolverine, animals that run hard and sleep hard, Petang's sleep was deep. Even shifting him to her other arm did not awaken him.

As she sat holding the beautiful wild thing, she scanned the water in the bottom of the pit until at last her eyes came to rest on the frog. His head was protruding above the surface of the water near the log.

"How," she said to Petang, "how do I catch him? Even so small a bite will keep you and me alive for another day. And tomorrow it might rain again and we can leave." She looked at the remains of the venison. "Half a meal for each of us. I'd better catch that frog."

A peal of thunder rumbled, and she looked up out of the pit. The sky was filled with rolling clouds; rain was indeed coming. She wouldn't have to catch the frog. The rumbling deluge would cool the soil, she hoped, and they could leave the pit today. She leaned back to wait for the thunderstorm to break, and then thought better of it. She had been fooled before. These were, after all, the years of the drought, and drought perpetuated drought. She eased Petang to the floor beside her deerskin pouch and carefully pulled out the hammock.

He did

not wake, and she smiled, cut off three feet of the hammock with her penknife and knotted the ragged ends so they would not unravel. She spread the net on the floor. Along one side she strung the heaviest of the shells and three long cords cut from the hammock ties. At the end of each cord she tied more shells. When she was done she had a fishnet, which she carried out on the log.

"Where are you, frog?" she asked. The wind trumpeted as it blew over the rim of the pit. Sparks exploded somewhere above her; but she did not heed them. Instead she concentrated on dropping the weighted end of the net across the deepest part of the pool. So that she could pull it up, she draped the cords over the log. The shells held them in place. Next she tied one corner of the unweighted side to a fig root on the wall, the other to a sapling on the other side of the pit. The net was set. Squatting, she poised herself to grab the cords and yank. The frog would have to come to the surface to breathe pretty soon, for he had been under a long time, and he was an air breather. With a swish, the sapling thrashed. Billie Wind grabbed the cords and pulled. Flopping in the net was a big large-mouthed bass.

"Petang," she shouted excitedly. "We will live. A fish, a fish." With a quick jab she thrust her fingers into the gills to make sure the bass did not escape, set the net again and ran back to the cave.

"We can live a long time down here, Petang," she said. "We have a bed, a fireplace, a cooking bowl—and food." She slit the fish from anus to gills with her penknife, removed the entrails and saved them for bait to catch other fish.

"Petang," she said to the still-sleeping otter. "How do you suppose a fish got down in this pit? He can not crawl on land or fly. Did a bird drop him? Did an egg wash in on a flood? Did the little underground men bring him here?" She smiled. "Little underground men are very useful. They explain all nature's mysteries." Then a thought occurred to her and she glanced around the cave.

"Do you suppose this was a fish pond for the ancients? Perhaps they brought them here eons ago. Perhaps a fish keeper lived in this cave. The Calusa cultivated fish, you know."

Petang smelled the entrails in his sleep and came awake. He bounced to Billie Wind's side.

"Here," she said, cutting off a large chunk of the tail. "You must learn to eat, not suckle." The otter tossed the food in the air, caught it and dug in with his teeth. Billie Wind put the remainder of the catch in the bowl with water from the pool.

"Now, how do I make a fire?" She glanced up at the top of the pit. "All that fire and no fire," she said, "but perhaps . . ."

Climbing to the last step of the sinkhole, she searched the embers until she found a flaming stick within reach. Licking her fingers she picked it up and backed down to the cave. To it she added chips from the log, whacked off with her machete. The chips caught fire.

When the coals were red she placed the ancient bowl carefully among them, hoping the old clay could still withstand fire. Then she squatted on her heels. The water bubbled, but did not boil. It must boil. She dropped a hot stone into the pot and the water rolled, then boiled, the fish simmered and the smoke climbed through the porous holes in the limestone ceiling of the cave.

"Petang," she announced when the fish was tender. "Dinner is served. And you are going to have nice soft fish to suckle." She need not have been concerned about this problem. The little otter had chewed and swallowed the uncooked tail of the bass and was sitting on his haunches, short front legs crossed on his chest, begging for more, cooked or uncooked.

Billie Wind held out a warm bite and watched him eat it with gusto and pleasure.

The sapling thrashed.

She put down her bowl and ran. Petang was close at her heels. What a mother otter does, a little otter does. Her next movements baffled him, however. She knelt down, reached out and pulled up a net. Then she lifted a fish above her head and cheered. Petang turned and scratched a flea.

"Fish," Billie Wind said addressing the bass. "Charlie Wind says that the animals talk. Tell me how you got here?"

The fish twisted in her hand. Its cold open mouth gave no answer.

Several days passed and the hot fires still burned. Each day Billie Wind would go to the surface hoping to be free, see that she was not, and climb down to play with Petang. They fished, slept and chased each other around the cave and up and down the log. Billie Wind laughed a lot at her funny little friend and dreamed of rain. When he slept she dug into the floor, uncovering more and more treasures.

One morning she dug up the beak of a sawfish. It resembled a double-edged saw almost precisely, and she wondered if it was strong enough to cut wood.

"Three-Hands-on-the-Saddle once cut limbs with a sawfish beak," she said to herself. "Maybe I can, too." She walked out on the log and drew the strange beak across one of the limb stubs. The ancient bone crumbled.

"No more of that," she said, putting it back where she had found it. "I am going to come back here someday. I will bring an archeologist and Charlie Wind, and they will look at all these things and tell me who the ancient person was and how the fish got into this hole on this island.

"Maybe the cave will give up a secret that will solve the mystery of where the Calusa came from."

That night she lay awake for a long time thinking of her ancestors and the daily lives they lived. They had fire and tools and fish and they made beautiful pots. The ghosts of the distant past seemed to snuggle closely around her, and she felt safe.

For two days no fish swam into the net.

"This is bad news, Petang," she said, the third morning. "I think we've caught all the fish there are in this hole, and the earth is still too hot for us to leave." Slowly she walked around the ledge at the water's edge, looking for dead snakes or turtles or even water beetles to eat.

The sapling jumped and she ran lightly, jumping rocks and holes to the net. She lifted it carefully. In it flopped a long-nosed garfish, which dwelled in the glades and was fed upon by the alligators. The fish was covered with a hard outer skin almost like bone. However, it could arch and flop, and it leaped out of the net onto the log. She threw herself upon it and wrapped it securely in her shirt.

Excited to see his mother on her belly, Petang ran up her back to her shoulders. There he looked down at the water. Although he had seen the water before, this time he really saw it. He leaned over and sniffed, then reached out and tapped it with his paw. It rippled. He struck it. It splashed. He leaned closer, put his head in, sneezed and pulled back. With his eyes he asked Billie Wind what it was all about. She was about to demonstrate the essence of water by splashing him, when some inherited gene told him what to do. He dove in headfirst and swam without instruction. It was as if he had been swimming since he was born. Circling and snorting water, he barked, rolled onto his back and took a back dive to the bottom. Up he came, chortling and whistling. Baubles of water clung to his whiskers.

"Petang, you're marvelous." Billie Wind exclaimed. "You are a water spirit." She reached out her hand to him; he climbed to her shoulder, turned and dove again. Shooting forward, he rounded the pool, leaped up into the air like a geyser and came to her. He tugged on her fingers.

"I get it. I get it," she said. "You want me to swim too, and I guess I'll have to. After all, I *am* your mother." Taking off her clothes, she held her nose and jumped into the pool with a splash that sent water sparkling up the walls of the pit. Then she rolled onto her back and kicked. Petang swam around her like a spinning, turning porpoise.

On the other side of the pool Billie Wind let her feet down. She could not touch bottom. The water was very deep. Petang sensed this, barked as if telling her to follow the leader, and dove deep. Billie Wind treaded water and peered down through the clear depths to see what he was up to. Surrounded with bubbles, he moved like a silver missile into an underwater cavern. She held her nose and went down to have a look.

The sun dimly illuminated the bottom, and she could see the bones of alligators and armadillos that had fallen into the pit and drowned. She recognized the skull of a black bear and a raccoon. Surfacing for a breath she went down again. She swam toward the cavern where Petang had gone, then turned back. It was too dark, its course too frightening; for it wound off under the pa-hay-okee, a river beneath the river of grass. Petang shot swiftly out of the darkness. In his mouth was a fish.

The two popped to the surface simultaneously and swam side by side to the log. Billie Wind pulled herself into the warm air and Petang leaped after her, holding tightly to his fish.

"Petang, you have told me how the fish got into the pit. When the glades dry up, the fish are not dead as we've always assumed; they are down in the underground pools and rivers waiting for the rains to return and fill the pa-hay-okee so they can come back to the saw grass.

"That seems so sensible I don't know why no one has thought of it before. Little underground men, ha." She reached for Petang's fish but he ran down the log and up the steps with it.

"Okay, okay," she called. "You can have it. I don't want your old fish. I have something important to do." She slipped into the water and swam back to the underwater cavern for one more look. Could it be, she wondered, that the ancients carved the tunnel from the sea to the pit to raise fish for the village? Was that why the steps were there? So the ancients could come down to the water and catch fish? She touched the walls and wished she knew more.

Clambering back onto the log she put on her clothes and looked for Petang. He was on the steps, swinging the fish from side to side.

"Come here," she said, stamping her foot. Petang dove into the pool. He surfaced, tossed the fish into the air and caught it before it escaped. Then he swam to the far side of the pit, crawled up on the ledge and stared across the water at her.

"If I didn't know better," she said, "I would say there is a naughty person inside that fur coat of yours." He sidled a few feet toward her, leaped into the water and came up on the log. She reached for him. Eyes shining, he ran into the cave, circled it twice, then dropped the fish and sat up on his haunches. He dangled his paws, his eyes black and lively.

"You are quite a playmate," she said, picking him up and hugging him. "It's very nice down here with you as a friend."

Billie Wind was cleaning the fish for dinner when Petang dove into the water, came out and shook all over her.

"Stop it!" she said. He shook again. She rocked back on her heels and stared at him. "Are you grinning, Petang? Do I see a smile on your face?

"No," she answered. "Of course, I don't. Otters don't tease people." She touched her head. "I've been down here too long."

Around noon the next day a wind blew across the island, plucking sad tunes on the burned tree limbs. Billie Wind climbed to the top of the pit to see if a storm was coming. The sky was clear. She despaired. She would never get out of the pit. Then she noticed that the loam had burned down to the bedrock. The soil was gone. It would take hundreds, maybe thousands of years for the plants to grow, die and build back the rich loam.

"I see why the scientists want to find other planets for us to live on," she said softly to no one in particular. "This one will soon be bare."

Nevertheless when she crawled into her bed that night and snuggled down with Petang, she was pleased that the fire had reached the bedrock. It could not burn anymore. She would soon be able to go home.

Billie Wind and Petang lived on the fish the otter caught in the underground river, and she watched the sky and waited. Every morning she climbed the steps to look across the forest floor, and with each trip she was cheered to see that one more fire had burned out. The ground became cooler and cooler. One morning as she came down the steps, she stopped and stared into the water. In the shallows near the cave entrance a bright green object shone.

"A plant," she said. "Petang, Petang, the sun is pulling life out of death."

Rolling up her pants, she waded onto the mud shelf and cut off the new shoot of a pickerel weed. The young leaves were pleasant to taste and Billie Wind ate them where she was, for she had not had green vegetables for many days; how many she did not know.

"Where did a plant come from in this burned world?" she asked herself. Reaching into the mud, she felt hard, round balls and brought them up.

"Seeds," she said. "Dropped by the birds who eat them?" She wondered how long they had lain there waiting for the sun: months, years, decades, perhaps. One question solved only presented another. This she did know: the seeds would never have sprouted had not the fire burned off the trees and let the sun into the pit.

"Nature plans ahead for her disasters," she said, reaching for another sproutling.

Before dusk that night Petang tumbled and boxed with Billie Wind until both were exhausted. They sat on the log to rest and cool off. Then Petang crawled into her lap as strange shadows raced over the pool and up the wall. Billie Wind looked up. A flock of wood storks was winging southward.

"The fire must be out," she said to Petang. "The wood storks are crossing over the island again." Petang was asleep, his paws folded on his chest.

"Is that what you are saying?" she asked the birds. Hardly had she spoken than a white heron alighted on the black limb of the dead oak above.

She stared at the bird for a long time, not daring to admit that it meant good luck; and yet she did think that and hoped that it was so.

As the sun came up the next morning Billie Wind heard thunder, opened her eyes and once more listened hopefully. She longed to be home with Mamau Whispering

Wind. She sat up and sniffed. The air smelled damp as it does before a rainstorm; but she had been disappointed too often to trust her nose. She lay back on her bed noticing Petang's nose twitching in his sleep.

"Do you smell rain, too?" she asked. "Your nose is twitching, and it is a much smarter nose than mine."

A lightning flash illuminated the cave. Billie Wind slipped from her bed and walked to the entrance. Bolt after bolt shot across the ruined forest. Petang joined her, whimpering at her feet. She picked him up and held him close.

"Why are you afraid? What do you know that I don't know? Tell me, please." An earsplitting thunder crack sent Petang leaping to the floor. He dove into her trouser leg. Billie Wind screamed, reached up, grabbed a ledge in the ceiling and dangled from it as she wildly kicked her foot, trying to dislodge the clawing, scrambling Petang. He fell to the floor. The ledge snapped, and Billie fell too. She covered her head as pebbles, dust and sand rained down upon her, but she did not move, for she was listening. Above the rifle shots of the thunder and the crash of stones a hiss could be heard.

"Rain," she said. "Petang, the rain is falling. Listen." The hiss turned to a hum, then a rumble, and the clouds above released their water in torrents.

After an hour of heavy rain with no letup in sight, she began to fear that the pool would rise and fill the cave.

"No," she said, recalling the ant lions. "They live in dry places." Nevertheless she and Petang huddled in the bedroom as high off the floor as they could get, listening until the rain slowed to a light patter.

She could leave. How glad Mamau Whispering Wind and Charlie Wind and Iron Wind and even Mary would be when she returned from the pa-hay-okee. Her eyes concentrated on the ledge in the ceiling that had broken under her weight. The corner of a square object stuck over the edge. She stepped out of bed, reached up and took down a dry leather pouch folded three times. It cracked when she opened it. A snake's fang fell out.

"A medicine bundle," she said in awe. "Petang. Where are we? What is this place?" Her spine tingled; then a buffalo horn fell from the pouch.

"Buffalo have not been here since the white men killed them all off to starve the Indians." She looked around slowly. "This is an old and important place." With care she replaced the fang and horn and put the medicine bundle back on the ledge.

"I must not disturb anything more. I will come back with people who will know what this place is."

The rain stopped. Hoping she would not be disappointed again, but afraid she might be, Billie Wind nevertheless climbed to the surface to test the rocks. They were cool. The once-red coals on the forest floor were black. Above the ravished island the sun was shining brightly.

"Petang," she called to the little otter, who was climbing up on the log from a fishless fishing expedition.

"We can go home. We can go home."

Swamp Talk

Billie Wind began packing her deerskin pouch after sorting over the ancient treasures and deciding which ones to take with her. The bowl, one cup, the hammer and the adz seemed to be good choices. They would convince almost anyone to follow her back to the mysterious cave. Next she pulled in her fishnet. A small bass flopped in it, and she decided to take the time necessary to render it to oil. She lit a fire and let it simmer until all the fat bubbled out.

Around noon she was ready to leave. Petang was nowhere to be seen. Running out on the log, she peered through the water to see if he was hunting in the cavern. A thin, piercing cry penetrated the air. She looked up. A red-shouldered hawk was perched on a limb of the blackened oak tree. His feathers were pressed close to his body and he was staring at the ground.

"What are you doing here, hawk?" she called. "Are you telling me that I am next on your menu? That I am the only living thing in this charcoal pit?" The stately bird's head turned away as his keen eyes followed a moving thing. Then he plunged. Petang came over the rim of the sinkhole.

"Hawk, Petang!" she warned. "Come down here." Waving her arms she ran up the steps. "Grrrr," she growled. "I am a snarling mother otter. Get out, hawk, get out."

Unperturbed, Petang bounded lightly down the steps carrying a snake in his mouth.

"So that is what the hawk is saying," she said upon seeing the snake. "He is saying that life is returning to the island; that the fires are out and that he is hunting here again."

Billie Wind was too excited by the prospect of going home to eat the snake, but not too excited to cook and wrap it in one of the leaves of the pickerel weed. She would take it with her for an emergency. Emergencies were a way of life these days.

When the fish oil was cool and thick she covered the bowl with bark from the log and placed it in the deerskin pouch with the rest of her possessions. She shouldered the pouch.

Without looking back she crossed the log and climbed up the steps. Petang bounced at her heels, happy to be following his mother anywhere.

Billie Wind stepped into the sunlight. She gasped. The island was completely destroyed. Rocks, ashes and blackened coals lay everywhere. The trees looked like dead men standing in their graves, arms reaching toward the Great Spirit. They saddened her.

A cry of sorrow for the trees and orchids and ferns came from deep within her as she stood in the cinders of the once beautiful island. Then out of nowhere came a host of yellow butterflies. They flew silently past her, their wings iridescent in the light. She watched them disappear among the dead things.

"Everything is all right," she said to Petang with a lilt in her voice. "Even the burned island. It's a dark pupa now, but it will burst into a beautiful butterfly in the sunlight and rain."

She gathered Petang in her arms and ran lightly around logs and burned debris to the dugout. It was a black ash.

"Fires," she said, "do not care about tribal dugouts. They are the same as a tree to the fire." She walked to the alligator moat and stared across its great width.

"There is no way off this island," she said. "I will be eaten alive if I swim." She scanned the surface for the eyes of the alligators, saw none and squatted on her heels to wait for a glimpse of a nose or a ripple that would tell her where they lurked. When Petang became restless she put him down.

"Go, little spirit," she said. "You can live here. This is your home. The snakes are back and the frogs are piping." She pushed his haunches with the palm of her hand to give him a start.

Petang braked and looked at her, his square face wrinkled as if with serious thought. Then he turned and bounced to the water's edge. There he looked back, whimpered, and rushed into her arms.

Laughing and crying, she buried her nose in his fur.

"I understand what you are saying. I am your mother. You and I can not part until you are grown up." She smelled the burned resin in his fur and, dipping the corner of her shirt in the water, wiped him clean with it.

"All right," she said. "We go together."

Billie Wind kicked through the ashes of the dugout until she found the steel head of the fish spear. With a sigh of relief at finding it, she put it in her pocket. At least she could spear fish on their trip home.

For almost an hour she watched the water for sign of alligators.

"Either they are all dead or they moved far out in saw grass away from the fire," she said. "Want to chance it, Petang? If I can get across this alligator moat to the saw grass perhaps I can see what to do next."

The water swirled. "Oh, no," she gasped and jumped

back. The rough back of a snapping turtle poked over the surface. Picking up a stick she threw it. He went under and swam away. She didn't like hungry snapping turtles either.

"It's now or never," she said and walked into the water holding her pouch on her head and Petang on the pouch. When the moat deepened, she trod water until her feet struck the rocks on the far side of the alligator moat. Quickly she scrambled into the saw grass, her leggings protecting her from the sharp stubble.

As she stood alone in the burned grass with the sun shining down on her, her clothes dripping, Billie Wind's thoughts went out to the island beyond the curve of the horizon: Panther Paw. Was her family alive? Had the fire reached them? Maybe. The land was black as far as she could see.

Across the sky winged a flock of white ibis. They bowed their wings deeply as they flew in the direction of Panther Paw. At the very rim of the horizon they dropped to earth.

"Thank you, ibis," Billie Wind said. "You have told me what I want to know. The grass is green where you are or you would not have come down. There are pools and insects and fish there. The fire did not reach Panther Paw." Putting Petang down, she turned slowly, looking at the devastation and here and there a new green shoot. At last she saw an island to the southwest.

"There it is, Petang," she said. "On that island is a tree, and that tree will be our boat."

The burn ended about one mile south of Cave Island, as Billie Wind now called it, for the wind had blown the flames northeastward. At the edge of the burn she stepped into the glorious green of the living grass, then turned around and looked back at Cave Island. She noted its position in respect to the other islands and memorized its contours so she could return to it. The island, she saw, now that it was denuded of the lush vegetation, had sloping sides and a flat top.

"It's an old village," she said in amazement, "built high and flat. And"—she now noticed strips of raised land leading out from the mound—"it had home sites and canals." The Calusas built their houses of reeds coated with ash and clay cement. They put them on poles on high land to keep them from being destroyed by the high water of hurricanes.

From this distance she could see faint depressions that had been the canals and fish ponds around the ancient village. Billie Wind knew that she had, indeed, found a rare spot in the wilderness.

"And no one will be able to bulldoze it down for houses, like they did the old ruins on Marco Island," she said. "Cave Island is deep in the pa-hay-okee, and no white man wants to live here among the alligators and mosquitoes in the steamy heat."

She strode toward the cypress island, feeling light-hearted. She had been released from her prison to live again. The Everglades' water glittered like quicksilver, and the birds flew in stringy flocks across the sky. She sang as she walked.

Up from the green, unburned grass came a cloud of mosquitoes. They covered her bare hands, neck and face. They pierced her flesh with their beaks and sucked up the blood they must have in order to lay their eggs. She knocked them off, swatted them, washed them in water. It was no use. They came on and on. Opening her pouch she took out the fish oil and spread it over her body, shirt and pants.

"It smells," she said to Petang, "but it keeps the mosquitoes away." He pawed the mosquitoes that were digging into the furless skin around his nose and eyes, so Billie Wind smeared his face with oil, too. He sneezed and pulled away. "You'll get used to it," she said. Petang sniffed and took another view of the oil. It was flavorsome. Eagerly he licked it from his nose and lips then sat up and begged for more.

"That's all you get if you are going to eat it," she scolded and walked hurriedly toward the island where her new hopes lay.

She splashed out of the water onto the cypress island to discover a grove of young sabal palms not far from the shore. They were the source of one of her favorite dishes, hearts of palm. She took out her machete, whacked down a small tree and cut the sweet white core out of the top of the trunk. She was pleased to see such an abundant crop. She pushed on. In a grassy meadow near the edge of the island languished the top-heavy fans of the saw palmetto. Each plant bore berries, and she was grateful for that, too. She ate handfuls as she passed among their shiny leaves searching for a place to hang the large part of her hammock that was not her net. At her heels bounced Petang, sniffing, investigating, pouncing and chirping with the excitement of many new smells. As she entered the cypress forest he slipped under a bromeliad and disappeared.

She folded her arms and looked over the forest. The trees were flared at the bases. This uncanny growth buttressed the cypress in the rainy season when the island was flooded with water and rendered the trees unstable. Near each tree jutted waist-high triangular "knees" that grew up from the roots. These breathed air when the roots were under water. Billie Wind walked among them until she found two slender trees that did not have buttresses.

"These trees are talking to me," she realized. "When the land is high and dry cypress trees do not grow buttresses. They grow straight like these. So the land is dry here. I have found a good camp ground.

"Petang," she called. "Where are you? We are going to camp here until our boat is made." The otter answered by rustling the palmettos and splashing into the water.

Billie Wind slung her hammock high. The species of mosquito that had been biting her did not fly higher than nine feet above the land, and so she would hang her bed at least ten feet high. To get up and down she braided a rope out of one of the many kinds of vines, tied it to the hammock and climbed up the tree. She secured the hammock.

Petang returned as she was putting the last stone on the fireplace. His sides were round and bulging.

"Goodness," she said. "You *have* been eating well. What's out there? Frogs? Fish?" She walked toward the shore to gather for herself whatever Petang had eaten.

A hiss sounded. The palmettos thrashed, and as Billie Wind jumped backward, she looked down on an enormous mother alligator who was escorting dozens of baby alligators down the side of a mound of humus, her nest. She turned back to help one hatchling who was still buried and peeping. Using her awkward-looking foot, she gently pulled back the black plants and let him climb out. A raccoon pounced on a baby at the bottom of the pile. She roared down on him, slashed her jaws and cut off his tail. He ran screaming into the brush. A heron flapped down and hovered over the tasty hatchlings. The mother alligator grunted and slammed her jaws, barely missing the bird, who rose higher to wait for another opportunity to strike. Roaring and snapping, the mother gator led her brood toward the safety of the water.

Billie Wind backed all the way home and climbed her rope to her hammock. She knew better than to stay anywhere near a mother alligator and her young.

Petang whimpered from the ground, and she climbed down the rope vine and picked him up. She tossed him into the hammock, stretched out and looked at the magical sunlight that made trees grow and alligators mate and lay eggs. Petang snored contentedly as she rocked high above mosquitoes and alligators. She thought of Mamau Whispering Wind and how happy she would be to see her.

The ibis screamed, the herons croaked, the frogs chirped, the egrets mewed. It was morning on the cypress head island. Billie Wind had forgotten how noisy the pa-hay-okee could be at dawn. She yawned and looked up through the mist to the treetops. They were soft and a red-gold color. They warmed her spirits and wiped away the pains of living. She rocked and watched.

As the rising sun burned off the mist she saw, hunched on the tree limbs above her, knotty old turkey vultures. Their necks were held forward and down so that their shoulders bulged above them. Their heads were red and naked and they stood two feet tall. They were waiting for the sun to heat the earth and the earth to heat the air and the air to rise and lift them into the sky. Once aloft they would float over the glades looking for the dead and dying animals upon which they fed. Billie Wind shivered, for she had escaped death so closely herself.

She slid to the ground to begin her day. The first thing on the list that morning was to cut a section from a bamboo stalk. To it she secured the spear head, then, passing the alligator nest after checking to make sure the mother was not around, she stalked a freshwater pond for frogs.

A harmless snake slid past her. She caught it, saw another and then another. There were an abnormal number of snakes and she wondered about them.

"The fire must have driven them here," she concluded. "Good," she added. "Food will be no problem." Snakes were a delicacy, sweeter than chicken. She would eat well while she made her boat. She watched the ground as she hunted frogs, keeping an eye out for the two very poisonous snakes that lived in the Everglades, the coral snake and the water moccasin. After some time she caught one big frog with her hands by sneaking up on it.

On her way back to camp she came upon a coconut palm and patted it affectionately. This tree was all things to the Indians; it was food, shelter, clothing, rope, fish netting, shade. The Indians planted them all over the glades. Since it leaned at an angle, she took off her shoes, placed her hands on the trunk and climbed like a monkey to pick one green and one brown nut. The others she would harvest when she needed them.

With a slash of her machete she opened the green one and drank the sweet coconut milk inside. Then she wedged off the brown husk from the other and put it aside to weave into ropes and mats. Finally, she cracked open the brown nut and dug out the fresh white meat. It tasted absolutely wonderful after her menu of fish and stalks.

Another snake writhed past her, and she cut off its head with a whack of the machete. The presence of so many snakes worried her and she looked for Petang. He was nowhere to be seen. She whistled, walked down to the water's edge and called. No Petang. On the way back to camp she gathered fuel for the fire, called again, stumbled and fell. She had tripped over a cypress log.

"A white heron must be flying over me," she said. "Here is my boat all felled and cut." The cypress forests had been logged years ago for the durable and valuable wood. It was old but not rotted, for cypress is practically indestructable.

Billie Wind cleared out the brush around it then tried to push it to the water. She could not budge it. "How will I launch my boat?" she asked herself, and not having an answer, went back to camp to think. She skinned the snake and frog and placed the biggest pieces in the bowl to simmer.

Once more she whistled for Petang. Silence was her answer. He would be along. She returned to the log with her machete and chopped until she had cut off the curving top of the log. Next she chipped one end, shaping it slowly into a pointed bow.

Late in the afternoon she called Petang again, for she had not seen him all day. His absence was disturbing. She ran to the water's edge to hunt for him. A water moccasin uncurled at her feet and slipped into the reeds. Now she was truly worried. Slashing her way through the brush with her machete, she called and searched. No Petang. She climbed a tree, scanned the ground, then looked out across the saw grass prairie toward her island.

Two buglike bulldozers were nudging the far end of

Cave Island. Horrified, she climbed higher hoping to find that it was only a mirage. It was not. The yellow machines snorted fuel-oil smoke, backed up, lowered their scoops and drove into the mound. Dust from the ancient shells enveloped them. She must run to them and tell them about the village. She must scream at them. She must . . . She could not move. And so she clung to the tree, crying, "Why? why? why? Why do you do this?"

Then she remembered the battle between the councilmen and the county officials. An airport was scheduled to be built near the Big Cypress Reservation.

"An airport."

She dropped to the ground and ran through the forest, jumping hummocks and logs as she returned to her boat. She chopped until nightfall, forgetting even about Petang. Miserable and bewildered, saddened, she climbed to her hammock by moonlight and lay awake staring up through the trees at the stars.

"You," she said to a distant star. "You are the one with a planet of water and grass and birds and little otters. I am leaving the pa-hay-okee and coming to you as soon as I can." Billie Wind finally rocked herself to sleep.

The next day she speared a fish for breakfast, cooked a heart of a palm and renewed her search for Petang. Had he found a home? Had he eaten a poisonous snake or toad? What had become of her friend? She needed him. She needed to cry into his fur and mourn for the staircase, the pit, the medicine bundle, the last traces of the last Calusas.

Sounds came from the end of the island. A male voice shouted, another yelled back. An airboat engine coughed and died. Was this island to be part of the airport too?

A shot rang out.

"Petang," she cried. "They've shot Petang." Frightened but desperate to know, she swung down from her hammock and tiptoed to a tall tree, climbed it, straddled a limb and looked down. Three men in hard hats were leaning over something on the ground. It flopped. Curling her head into her chest to cover her eyes, she sat still for a long time. Then the airboat engine started up and roared across the saw grass toward what remained of Cave Island.

Slowly she walked back to camp. She did not care anymore. Even to return home seemed to be too much of an effort. She could not get the cypress log in the water, Cave Island was demolished, Petang was dead and there were no spaceships to take her to that bright star with its gentler planet.

She threw herself facedown on the ground and her fingers touched Mamau Whispering Wind's deerskin pouch.

"I'm not going to make it after all, Mamau," she cried. "Even your help was not enough."

The pouch moved. She stared at it. It leaped. The flap lifted and Petang thrust his head out, his eyes bright and inquisitive.

Billie Wind gathered him up in her arms and laughed until he bit her in annoyance. Putting him down she took up the adz, carved a handle for it and went back to the log. Standing atop it, she swung the ancient tool over her head and brought it down with a crack on the cypress wood. With steady blows she chopped a hollow in the log.

Later in the day she watched Petang drag a gopher tortoise toward the water, presumably to drown it. It was too heavy for him, and Billie Wind laughed out loud, amused at his feeble effort to move the tortoise along.

"Now you know how I feel," she said. "I can't move this log."

The little otter did not give up. He bounced from one side of the tortoise to another, sized up the situation and then he began to dig. He dug a deep long canal. It filled with water and Petang floated the tortoise down it to the moat, and there drowned his prey.

"Well," said Billie Wind, "that is talking if I ever heard it. You have just told me how to launch my boat. I, too, will dig a canal and float the dugout into the pa-hay-okee. By golly, Charlie Wind, the animal gods really *do* talk."

Billie Wind chopped the log and shaped its ends so that it would be buoyant like a leaf. All day her machete flashed or her adz rose and fell. When the sound of the bulldozers reached her ears she chopped louder and harder.

Sometimes she stopped and simply dreamed of home. The Green Corn Dance festival was long over, the games played out. Many of the people of Panther Paw would have returned to their homes on the Big Cypress Reservation, and Iron Wind might be working at the Kennedy Space Center again, for all she knew.

One evening she crawled into her hammock early. Petang had adopted the deerskin pouch as his bed, preferring shelter on the stable ground to the swinging hammock. She watched the star around which her pretty planet spun. It would not have mosquitoes or snakes. If it did, she would jet off and find another. It was fun to fly in her imagination among the stars. If she did not like one planet she went to another.

A raindrop struck her face. She had nearly forgotten about rain. Sliding to the ground she picked up a mat she had woven from the leaves of the coconut palm, tied it around her waist and carried it aloft.

Hardly had she settled under her rain shelter than she heard a coarse rattle in the treetop. A snake in the tree? She peered up. A raccoon was descending headfirst, a baby in her mouth. The little one was curled like a bean. The mother reached the ground, walked into the underbrush and after a long time climbed back up and came down with another kit.

"Why are you moving your babies?" Billie Wind asked. "Where are you taking them? I don't like the wild things to move. They only move when something terrible is about to happen—like a fire."

She watched the mother shuffle off into the darkness. An alligator bellowed an alarm call. Billie Wind wished her boat was finished and that she and Petang were on their way home.

When she awakened in the morning she was disturbed to see that the vultures who were her morning companions were not in their roost.

"I don't like this at all," she said, swinging down to the ground on her rope. She ate a hasty breakfast of coconut rind and boiled conte fern roots before noticing that the mosquitoes were not swarming. She shook the leaves of a palmetto. No crickets or grasshoppers leaped into the air.

"Now I know what the animals are telling me," she said. "The white men have sprayed. The white men spray chemicals to kill the mosquitoes before they work a place. It is time to leave."

Gathering bark and sticks she hurried to the dugout. A fire would burn a hollow in the boat faster than she could chop. When she had arranged the oily bark of the coconut under some sticks she took out her magnifying glass and held it so that the sun shone through it; and in a few seconds the bark smoked and burst into flame.

Two days later she chipped the last of the charred wood from the inside of the dugout. Then she lifted her adz and swung it into the ground to begin the canal to the water. When she knocked out the last foot of soil the water rushed in, the canal filled, the boat rocked to the surface and she easily pushed it into the river of grass.

It floated like a leaf. Cheering aloud she climbed in and rocked it. It was quite stable.

"Petang," she called. "It's time to go." Whistling for

him, she ran back to her camp, took down the hammock and once more packed her possessions in her deerskin pouch. This time she had more things to carry: two mats she had made, and a dozen coconuts, the heart of a palm and berries. She loaded them all in the boat.

"I saw her yesterday." A man was speaking. Billie Wind startled and stood up. Someone was not far away. Prickles of fear ran through her arms and legs.

"Why don't you leave her alone?"

"Aw, I just want to talk to her." He laughed coarsely and all the Seminole stories of battles with the white man rushed to Billie Wind's mind like a nightmare.

She glanced around for Petang. He was not in sight. Picking up her pouch, crouching so as not to be seen above the wall of palmettos, she glided to her dugout.

The men were now at the edge of the island picking their way through the rushes and grass. She dared not whistle for Petang—or wait for him. Slipping quietly into her boat, she grabbed the overhanging bushes and pulled herself into their cover. She moved the boat slowly so as not to ripple the water.

She wondered what to do next. In minutes they would find the warm coals of her campfire and the chips of wood from her boat lying fresh on the ground. They would then know to look for her on the water.

"Help!" The voice was agonized and frightened. "Pat. Pat. Where are you? Water moccasin bit me. Pat!" Feet pounded the ground as the other man came running to him.

"Don't move. Slash the wound with your knife. Make it bleed. I'll go to the airboat and radio for help."

Billie Wind could hear the second man run toward the boat and the moans and cries of the snake-bitten man told her he would not be looking for her. She was free.

"Thank you, snake," she said and, standing up in the boat, poled swiftly around the island and out across the pa-hay-okee. She wanted to be far away when the helicopters arrived to administer aid to the stricken man.

She could not go home the way she had come, for white men were everywhere. She steered her boat toward Big Cypress Swamp, knowing that it was laced with rivers that flowed southward to the Ten Thousand Islands. On some of these rivers were tribal islands like Panther Paw. She would paddle and pole and even sail if she had to, until she found her own people.

Leaning hard on her pole she skimmed the dugout over the sunlit waters of the pa-hay-okee. The shining stalks of the saw grass were reflected upside down with the clouds. The air was hot and humid. She poled with all her energy, grieving for Petang but too frightened to turn back.

A mile out her arms refused to work. She could not lift the pole even one more time.

"Petang," she sobbed, "I can not leave you." Turning around, she pushed the boat back to the island, docked on the western side and covered the dugout with her palm mats for camouflage. The clatter of a helicopter sounded in the distance. She crawled under the mat. The fat hornetlike machine came closer and closer. The trees pranced as it whirled overhead. With a rumble it came down on the far side of the island.

The rescuers' voices were muffled by the heat of the noon air. Finally the engines roared and the helicopter arose and clattered toward Fort Myers and the hospital. She held her breath waiting for the airboat to start up. A cough and a snort announced its start, and its whining whir faded into the distance as it sped toward the ruins of Cave Island.

She peered out from under the mat, tossed it back and hopped ashore. On silent panther feet she ran to her campsite. Petang was not there. He was not at the canal, not in the roots of the tree where he often went to keep cool.

Thoughtfully she returned to her boat. "He *is* a grown-up otter," she reminded herself, trying to be practical, "and it is time he went off to seek his fortune." She slipped under the mat and curled into a ball. Too tired to pole out into the pa-hay-okee, she pushed the pouch under her head and closed her eyes. Her fingers touched something wet and cold. She sat up.

"Petang," she scolded. "You are a terrible little man who plays tricks on bad Seminole children. Where have you been? Have you been asleep in the bow of this boat all the time?" She gathered him up in her arms and held him close. His body was wiry and strong now, and he was as heavy as a sack of corn. He was indeed getting big. "You are wicked." She laughed and scratched him under the chin. He licked her cheek. "And wonderful." She slept until the moon came up.

A bobcat caterwauled from far, far away. A fox yipped. Billie Wind lifted the mats and sat up.

"I hear you, animals." she said. "You talk very well. It's just that I don't understand you. But I know you are telling me something important. Something very, very important." She found her star in the domed sky. "I will listen until I know what it is.

"I resolve here and now not to leave the beautiful pa-hay-okee until I can tell Charlie Wind what you are saying."

Coootchobee

 As the crooked moon climbed the sky the next night Billie Wind poled into Big Cypress Swamp. The giant trees closed behind her like a protective door as she followed a slow river into the forest. The waterway was a pale path leading through the dark shadows. She pushed on and on.

"The deeper the better," she said, still feeling the pain of the bulldozers crushing Cave Island and her fear of the men who had tracked her. Gradually her shoulders relaxed and pleasant thoughts came to her. On the silver river frogs sang lazy songs. A gray fox barked somewhere in the forest and bats dropped out of the trees and spun over the water catching bugs. The mood here was gentle.

"I can hear what these animals are saying, Petang," she said to the otter, who shifted against her foot. "They are saying: 'All's well. You and the little otter are safe here with us.' "

Alligators stoically watched her pass, their eyes like jewels set in knotty sockets. To Billie Wind they were no longer frightening. The gators were members of the swamp community with rights like hers and Petang's to live and eat and grow and die.

The boat struck an island that supported an enormous cypress tree, braced with gigantic buttresses. She grabbed a knee on which grew a garden of plants that eat animals. Pitcher plant was their name, for the flowers were shaped like pitchers even to the lips. Their sweet odor attracted insects who walked down the lips into the pitcher, never to come out again. Down-turned hairs eased them in, but stabbed them when they tried to climb back.

Billie Wind tied the boat to the knee with its sinister crop and stretched out on the bottom of the dugout. The barred owls called, the raccoons chittered and the swamp night enveloped her like the loving arms of Mamau Whispering Wind; and she fell asleep.

The morning sun was as soft as candlelight, for it was filtered by curtains of Spanish moss, air plants and the lacy leaves of the cypress trees. She opened her eyes to the smell of decay: swamp odor, as sweet as the plants it came from.

A pileated woodpecker, who was as big as a crow,

alit on the trunk of the tree to which she was tied and instantly chipped off a four-inch chunk of wood with her sharp beak. The chip hit Petang. Annoyed, he moved to the bow of the boat and promptly went back to sleep. Billie Wind leaned over the edge of her dugout and peered into the water.

"Bass," she said to the sleeping Petang. He awoke, put a paw over one eye, peered out with the other and lay still. She tickled his webbed foot.

"Get up. The fish are too deep for me to spear. You must catch one." He slid back to the deerskin pouch and closed both eyes.

"All right, all right. I'll catch frogs for breakfast . . . and I'll eat every bite myself." She picked up her spear and climbed out on the cypress mound, where she found not only frogs but the nest of a turkey vulture. She took one of two eggs, knowing that the bird would lay another. Most birds do not sit on their nests until the females have the right number of eggs to incubate. The turkey vulture required two.

She made a small fire on the riverbank, boiled the frog meat and egg, then stepped into the bow of the boat to eat. Nearby was a cluster of sundew plants. They, like the pitcher plants, were carnivorous greenery that ate living creatures. Their flowers looked like two open hands rimmed with tiny fingers. Presently a fly sat on one, and the brainless plant closed upon it. The many spikes intertwined like fingers, and locked. When they opened there was no fly, just chitin, the exoskeleton.

"How did that plant come to be?" Billie Wind asked all the living things around her for she was awed by what seemed to be some kind of intelligence in a plant. She dropped a bit of dirt in the open palms. They closed, then quickly opened to reject the dirt. She looked up through the trees toward the invisible star. "Will the new planet have a miraculous sundew plant growing on it?" she mused. "Will it? For it will be dull there without one."

In the swamp, time had no minutes or hours, just years and ages, and so Billie Wind felt the timelessness, and it was not until late in the afternoon that she untied her boat and drifted on down the river, going somewhere she did not know. The river widened, narrowed, turned; taking her, it seemed, into the very soul of the swamp where all answers must lie.

That evening she tied up beside an island and climbed up a small hill to sleep above the mosquitoes. A family of armadillos rooted noisily in the leaves, and two raccoons fought over a fish in a pool. But she did not mind the noises. The swamp was an enormous shelter, and Billie Wind felt safe.

One morning she poled around a bend and came upon a line of wooden posts and iron rails half submerged in the black water. The posts led off into the forest, and Billie Wind recalled stories of the lumberjacks who had lived in Big Cypress Swamp, cutting down trees and shipping them out on rail trains. When the last of the giant trees were felled the men had departed. The rails rusted and fell into the muck and the woodpeckers drilled holes in the posts. The swamp claimed all things man made, leaving only the durable cypress wood. Near the posts, stumps nine feet in diameter remained intact to tell the story of a once amazing forest of trees.

Jammed against one of the posts was an old wooden crate blackened by the tannin from the decaying leaves in the water. Billie Wind pulled it aboard.

A brown pelican came around the bend, winged down the river and disappeared.

"What are you doing here?" she asked the boat-bodied pelican. "You are a bird of open water." Petang sat up on his haunches and pawed the air. "The pelican tells me we are coming to a lake, Petang. But you already know it." She laughed and picked him up.

A low hissing swelled into a rumble. Billie Wind dropped to her belly. She had had too many bad experiences with strange sounds not to take precautions. The sound softened and she lifted her head.

"Bird wings," she exclaimed. Before her was a vast shallow lake, where thousands and thousands of wood storks, egrets, ibis and herons were beating their wings as they took off for the day to hunt the pa-hay-okee.

"A rookery," she said when she saw clusters of stick nests high in the trees. She thought about omelettes and boiled eggs.

From the middle of the lake she could see an abandoned cabin in the forest. A broken dock sat in the water in front of it. She wondered if they had been built by the lumberjacks.

"No," she said, seeing its proximity to the rookery. "That is a plume hunter's camp." Mamau Whispering Wind's mother had told her of the plume hunters who shot almost all the snowy egrets for their beautiful plumes.

"Once the sky was white with birds," the old woman had said. "Once the pa-hay-okee flowered with them. Then one day they were all gone except a few that roosted near the Indian villages. Finally the white man passed a law against killing birds and the plume hunters were arrested or went away. Over the years the Indian birds had young and their young had young. Now there are many birds. But the pa-hay-okee will never see the great numbers again because the white men also cut down the nesting trees and drained the glades. There is not enough food for great numbers of birds anymore."

Billie Wind poled to the plume hunter's dock, tied up her boat and stepped ashore. The cabin was simple: a door, a window, walls and a roof. She went inside. Leaves were blown into the corners, a floorboard wobbled. It was not nailed down. She picked it up, carried it to the dock, then went back for another. When she had seven wide boards she floated a log against her dugout and placed the boards across both of them. She lashed them down with vines.

"A houseboat," she said when the floor was done. Petang, who had been swimming and fishing, came up a plank she had laid for him and ran in circles on the new floor.

"I think we are going to be traveling for a long, long time," she said, "and we might as well be comfortable."

The next morning she strapped four posts to the corners of the platform with wire she found near the cabin. Bamboo poles made a frame for the roof.

Before the sun went down she set out for higher land to gather the leaves of the sabal palm. The next day she laid these on the framework, one upon the other like shingles, until she had a thick waterproof roof.

When it was done she gathered orchids and bromeliads from the trunks of the trees and hung them from the eaves of her houseboat. They reminded her of green stars as they stirred in the breeze.

"Beautiful," she said with great satisfaction. "Petang, we have a home."

Too tired to boil bird eggs for dinner, she ate one raw, tossed Petang a frog she had caught and poled her houseboat out into the middle of the shallow lake. There she strung her hammock between two roof supports, crawled in and fell instantly asleep.

Yatter, reee, reee, reeee. At first she thought a hysterical woman was screaming somewhere from deep within the swamp. Petang, who was sleeping in his pouch below, woke up and shivered.

"Who is it?" she said, leaning down. "You know, but you can't talk." He thrashed his paws; she leaned over and lifted him into the hammock beside her.

Yatter, reee, reee. The animal person screamed in human-like horror. The frogs stopped piping, the owls did not hoot, the swamp sounds ceased to be. Billie Wind lay wide awake.

When she finally fell asleep she dreamed that a star person from the planet of her distant sun dropped into the swamp and came to her houseboat. He spoke in whimpers and grunts like Petang, but in her dream she understood every snorting word.

"Come to my faraway planet. You will not be punished for doubting up there. I am in the forest. Come find me."

When she awoke in the morning she lay very still recalling her dream, for it had been very real. Charlie Wind had said that the Seminole Indian dreams should be heeded and obeyed.

"I must go find the star person," she concluded. "He has come to take me to the planet. He is in the swamp behind the cabin."

She poled quickly to the plume hunter's dock. Petang slid down the ramp and splashed into the water, barked and swam off among the reeds. Billie Wind stepped ashore with hesitation, for she was not certain she wanted to meet the star person.

In the grass at her feet was the tip of an iron pancake griddle. Glad for an excuse to do something else, she dug it up and put it down in the middle of the houseboat for a fire box. She spent a long time carrying stones, which she put on the griddle for a pot rack. That done,

she was perfectly satisfied to walk around the house looking for other utensils for her houseboat rather than hunt
the star person. She found an iron teapot, a grill and
the bottom of a chair.

Yatter, reee, reeeee, reee.

Billie Wind stared into the forest. Petang sped up the
ramp and dove into the crate.

"Dreams are very important," she repeated and, gathering her courage, taking a deep breath, walked into the
dark swamp of forest. She leaped from grass hummock
to grass hummock. A strap fern danced wildly as if hiding
someone. She dropped to her hands and knees and peered
around it.

Between two trees a golden spider was spinning a
golden web. Nothing else was there. She ran back to
the dock and poled the houseboat far out into the shallow
lake. That night she slept on the floor under the palm
roof so as not to see the stars.

Around daylight she heard the bloodcurdling scream
again. She sat up. The boat had drifted into the reeds
during the night, and the voice was almost upon her.
Jumping to her feet she picked up her pole and was pushing back to the middle of the lake when a huge beast
leaped over the reeds and stopped still.

"A coootchobee," she gasped. "Petang, the star person
is a panther. Panthers are rare. Mamau Whispering Wind
says they are almost gone from this earth." She was happy
to see the panther but also frightened, and she leaned
heavily on her pole. The panther, screaming half in in-

quiry, half in temper, sprang at Billie Wind, missed the boat and fell into the water. The animal, a she-panther, was dark in color, the size of a Great Dane but much more compact and muscular. She swam toward the houseboat.

Billie Wind could not pole fast enough to get away. Frantically she picked up her machete and raised it above her head.

A loud clap sounded. Water splashed as high as the roof. The panther screamed and went under. An alligator tail seven feet long whipped past Billie Wind's face and sank below the water surface.

And then there was silence.

Billie Wind got down on her knees and peered into the murky water. Although shaking from her narrow escape, she was nevertheless sad over the fate of the beautiful Florida panther.

"Petang," she said softly to the otter, who was still in the crate. "The coootchobee is dead. I cry for her."

Yatter, reeee, reeee. Billie Wind dove into the crate with Petang, and for hours they listened to the ghoulish cry of the she-panther's mate, calling from the black shadows of the swamp.

"He is so sad," Billie Wind said to Petang as they ate their lunch. "I think he knows his mate is dead. But how?" The mystery of animal communication filled her with respect. That night she slept restlessly, awakening at each cry and wishing she could help the heartbroken animal.

The sun climbed the sky. By the dozens and hundreds of dozens the wood storks, ibis, and egrets flew off to the pa-hay-okee. Their beating wings whitened the trees as they departed in tattered streams. Then they were gone, all but one old bird who did not have the energy to fly. He was standing by the water. Suddenly an alligator flashed open its mouth and swallowed him. Billie Wind thought about that.

Later, when the birds had departed, she poled ashore and cut reeds, laid them in straight lines on the floor of the houseboat and, picking a cattail leaf, wove it in and out. All day her fingers flew until she had a strong, sweet-scented mat, then she began another. While she worked, Petang slid down his board, chased dragonflies, tossed fish in the air and snorted at turtles.

The sun went down. The sun came up. Clouds came and clouds blew away. By day the water was as blue as the sky. The moon turned it silver at night.

One morning the reeds along the shore plunged up and down so vigorously that Billie Wind poled in to see what was the matter. The stalks rustled and a panther kitten splashed into the shadows. He was fuzzy with yellow-brown fur elaborately spotted with black.

"A baby," she said. He wrinkled his nose and mewed pitifully. Billie Wind ran down the plank, waded to the beautiful creature and gathered him up in her arms. He did not fight or protest.

"Coootchobee," she said, snuggling him against her chin. "Your Mamau Whispering Wind is dead. I will take her place." Lifting his head she looked into two round yellow eyes set in a gold-and-black face. Although he was young he already wore the hallmark of the American panther, or mountain lion: black mask, nose bridge and cheek patches. He was about three months old, Billie Wind guessed when she saw his baby canine teeth and cuspids. He spat fiercely for a few minutes, then sniffed her face and licked her chin. His tongue was warm and rough.

Billie Wind carried him back to the houseboat stroking his head as his mother would have done, mewing to him and talking to him in housecat sounds, for that was the only cat language she knew. Sitting on the floor in the shade of her palm roof she rocked the big kitten tenderly. His ears twitched, his eyes rolled and then he began to purr. He purred louder and louder, his whole body vibrating with the solo; then he sighed and fell asleep.

"Petang," Billie Wind whispered. "How will I get enough food for this huge baby? The deer are too big for my spear. The fox squirrels climb too fast. The opossums hang on twigs too slender to climb. The armadillos dash into the ground. The bears are too big and the raccoons too clever to catch." She thought a moment. "And if that isn't bad enough, the swamp rabbits jump into the water and swim away." She looked at the kitten, then slowly focused her eyes on Petang, who was lying on his back in the crate, his head turned so he could see and hear her.

"You!" she exclaimed. "You will catch fish for Coootchobee."

Petang, however, had his own views on the panther kitten. He dashed out of the crate, nipped the sleeping Coootchobee on the ear and ran back.

"Why, you're jealous," she scolded, then laughed as Petang eyed his rival and sulked.

"Well, forget you for a provider," she said and recalled the old stork that the alligator had so easily caught. She put the kitten down, picked up the pole and pushed the houseboat across the lake and tied it under the trees of the rookery.

"Almost every day a bird dies," she said to Coootchobee. "You might as well have them as the gators."

After a long wait a lone bird stepped daintily to the water's edge. His feathers were rumpled, his wings drooped. She clapped her hands. The bird drew back but did not fly. Lifting her spear she aimed at the ibis. An alligator surfaced a few feet from the dying bird. Billie Wind broke off a stick and threw it at him, and the gator disappeared beneath the water. Billie Wind tossed her spear swiftly and accurately. She jumped ashore and picked up the bird.

Climbing aboard she saw that Coootchobee was still asleep, but that Petang was gone. She hoped he had not deserted her because she had adopted the panther. She placed the food beside the big kitten and sat down to her weaving.

Up the plank came Petang, and, fur dripping, he sidled

up to her. With a snort he shook water all over her. Billie Wind laughed out loud and snatched up the jealous otter. She held him close, touching his soft lips with her finger tip.

"I admire Coootchobee," she said. "But, Petang, I love you." He grunted.

Swamp Rivals

Billie Wind swung out of her hammock the next morning to hunt food for Coootchobee. She whistled for Petang to go with her. He sulked in his crate, paws over his eyes; and so she stalked the rookery alone.

After an hour's search and having found nothing but a frog, she started back to the houseboat to fish with her net. Near a tree root a muskrat left his door for the water, and with a thrust of her arm she deftly speared it.

"Forgive me, Otobee," she said in the manner of her

ancestors who asked the animals they killed for forgiveness.

"Charlie Wind," she said. "You should hear me now. It is not the animals who are talking to me, but I who am talking to the animals." She smiled at herself and waded back to Petang and Coootchobee. After lighting a fire on her iron hearth, she skewered the frog on a reed and turned it slowly over the flame. Petang opened his eyes.

"Come out, little otter," she called. "Don't sulk. The coootchobee is nice." She held out a hot morsel of food to the otter but he tucked his head into his belly and curled tighter.

"Like it or not, Mr. Petang," she said, "we are going to save this kitten. And I shall tell you why."

"Many years ago when the Earth was young and the adopted son of the Corn Mother was a boy who ran through the woods and hunted in Big Cypress Swamp, he met a gray wolf.

" 'Who are you?' the wolf asked. Those were innocent days when men thought the animals talked to people," she said by way of explaining to herself why she was having the animals speak.

" 'I am the adopted son of the Corn Mother,' he replied.

" 'What are you doing?'

" 'I am hunting a deer.'

" 'But only I can hunt deer,' replied the wolf. 'You and I are rivals. One of us must die.'

"The wolf snarled. The adopted son of the Corn Mother raised his spear, only to remember he had cracked it while hunting an alligator. He hesitated. The wolf lunged, but as he did so, a panther dropped from a tree and killed the wolf.

"And so the Calusa and Seminole Indians have always befriended the panther."

Petang dug his nose deeper into his chest.

"Now it's my turn to save the panther," she said. "And you, little fisherman, are going to help me." She lifted him out of the crate and held him against her cheek. "I hope."

The otter's hair rose on his back at the sight of the sleeping Coootchobee. He wriggled out of her arms, hit the water and swam off, snorting as he glided toward shore. He did not look back or show any sign of cooperating with Billie Wind at all.

"You are a funny otter-person," she called.

Later in the morning she speared a rabbit for Coootchobee. His hunger satisfied, she laid sabal leaves on the floor and wove them into a bed for the panther. She was concentrating so hard that she did not notice a storm moving their way.

A sudden flash of lightning lit up the lake. Thunder boomed. Petang came out of the water, ran up the plank and dove into his crate. He growled at the kitten.

With a roar the rain poured down. The wind blew it sideways, drenching Billie Wind and Coootchobee. They crawled into the crate with Petang. He snarled at the panther kitten, then crept up on Billie Wind's shoulder. He laid his head against her ear.

"Well, here we all are," she said, smoothing the bristling fur on Petang's back. "We might as well get along with each other."

Coootchobee knew a rival when he saw one. He reached with his enormous paw and batted the otter. Billie Wind turned sideways to keep the rivals apart. The thunderstorm raged on, raising the water of the lake and bringing the birds back to the rookery to protect their eggs and offspring.

Cramped and miserable, Billie Wind dared not move until Petang stopped snarling at the kitten and the kitten stopped trying to biff Petang. After a long time, sometime in the middle of the night, when the thunder ceased and the rain stopped falling, Petang extended his neck, sniffed Coootchobee and licked his cheek. The kitten meowed and the panther and the otter came to terms with each other.

"Well," she said happily, "I am now the mother to an otter and a panther. The otter is a father to the panther and the panther is a son to the otter and me.

"Even I believe only a medicine bundle could conjure up this family." She hugged the big kitten and kissed Petang. "But all living things are a family, and one can not live without the other."

In the morning when the last of the birds were gone from the rookery, Billie Wind walked to the stern of her boat and studied the shoreline. Seeing a feeble ibis hunting the waterline, she stalked and speared the dying creature for Coootchobee.

She skinned this bird before letting the panther have it and hung the beautiful white mantle to dry in the sun.

"I don't know how long we are going to be here feeding this big kitten, Petang," she said to the otter, "but I need a new shirt, and bird skins make gorgeous clothes."

After three or four days the food and loving care assured Coootchobee that Billie Wind was a friend, and he relaxed and began to romp. One afternoon Petang brought a bass from the water and dropped it on the floor near Coootchobee who sniffed, bit it and found the taste was good. He gobbled it down and licked his jaws.

"Good news," Billie Wind said as she sewed three bird skins together in a circle and put them over her head. "Coootchobee can live on fish." She smoothed the white feathers and turned around for her friends to see.

"This is my traveling suit," she said. "Coootchobee is eating fish. We do not need the rookery anymore. It is time to move on."

The next day Billie Wind readied her houseboat for the trip to the sea. She gathered armloads of dry firewood, hung mats so that the rain would not blow in and put fresh palm leaves in the crate for Petang and Coootchobee to sleep on.

The Calusa bowl she placed beside the hearth with the conch cups, adz, hammer and machete. The fishnet and spear she laid on the floor near the bow of the boat ready for action. Then she waded into the shallows and gathered dozens of the potatolike tubers that grow on the roots of the arrowhead plants. She stored them in the iron teapot she had found near the cabin.

Early that afternoon the floating house moved across the shallow lake, casting a strange reflection. An Indian girl, a panther, an otter and a chickee rode right side up and upside down upon the mirror of the water.

At the far side of the lake Billie Wind searched for an exit. There should be a river or canal flowing toward the sea. The water, however, seeped off through the tall trees without forming a river. There was no exit.

"The lumberjacks and plume hunters got their loot out of here somehow," she said, and poled to the western side of the lake to have a look.

"The railroad," she said. "Of course. But it has decayed and rusted." Petang, who was sitting on top of the crate cleaning his fur with his tongue, stopped and twitched his ears at her.

"We are locked in here, Petang. Tell me what to do. You know the ways of water. When we were starving in the cave you found the underground stream and fish for us to eat. Now give me a clue as to how to get out of here."

The otter scratched and went back to his grooming. Billie Wind poled slowly around the lake until dusk, poking among the reeds searching, searching. When the stars shone she gave up the hunt for an outlet, and climbed into her hammock to sleep.

"The cabin," she said, sitting up. "I saw a map burned on the wall of the plume hunter's cabin. It could be he mapped a way out."

In the morning she poled to the dock and ran to the house. The winding river by which she had entered the lake was clearly drawn on the wall. She recognized the turns. About a quarter of a mile north a straight line was drawn southeastward from the river.

"A canal," she said, recognizing the mechanical look of the manmade waterway. "And it leads to the Fahkahatchee Slough, and the slough runs into a river that leads to the Ten Thousand Islands in the Gulf of Mexico."

The trip upriver was difficult for the rains had raised the water level and the current was swift, but late in the afternoon Billie Wind found the canal the plume hunter had mapped. It was so overgrown that it was barely wide enough for her houseboat. Fallen trees blocked the course and she was often forced to chop or push them aside. After many days of hard work she reached the Fahkahatchee Slough.

She knew she was off the canal when the water deepened and flowed naturally in meandering twists, and when the forest birds were replaced by the water birds. Dark, chickenlike coots with white bills and rumps swam among the water plants; gallinules dove for food, their feathers shedding bright drops of water when they surfaced. A bittern warned Billie Wind not to come any closer to her nest in the tall sedges. "I won't. I won't," she replied, bending down to peer through the stalks and glimpse the long-necked babies. The bird quieted down when she had passed.

Petang found the fishing excellent and generously brought fish aboard for Coootchobee, who would bat them across the floor when they flopped. One morning the kitten became so excited he struck Petang. The power of the young panther was astounding. Petang was lifted into the air and came down three feet away. He turned angrily on the playful panther. Coootchobee misunderstood and, still playing, enveloped him in his paws and rolled over and over. Clenched in the strong grip, Petang bit. The kitten screamed, dropped the otter and got to his feet.

"Poor Coootchobee," Billie Wind said, gathering the panther in her arms and stroking his head. She turned to Petang and shook her finger.

"No biting," she said, and tapped his nose. That did it. He snorted and ran into the crate.

A mile or so down the slough Billie Wind recognized an orange and an avocado tree poking over the bushes along the shore.

"An old Indian campsite," she conjectured, pushing the houseboat laboriously toward them. Leaping ashore she climbed the trees and gathered all the oranges and avocados that were ripe, then struggled through the bushes behind the campsite to where she knew a dump would be. Springing up from a mound, as she suspected, were squash and beans and other plants that had grown from the seeds the hunters had thrown away with their garbage.

That night she made a fish stew with vegetables and served it to her companions and herself. Dinner over, she fashioned a broom from the stiff roots of a conte plant and swept her houseboat clean. She watered the orchids, pausing to watch a hummingbird inspect the red flower of an air plant. A butterfly flew to the crate and rested. She tidied the mats and arranged her pots, then sat down by her hearth, hugging her knees and feeling proud of her own little spaceship.

At sunup the next morning Coootchobee awoke and stretched. His big paw touched the Calusa bowl. It teetered. Fascinated that the object had come to life, he tapped it. It wobbled. Billie Wind heard the noise and looked down too late. The panther kitten gave the bowl a mighty swat. It shot across the floor, hit the post and smashed into pieces.

"No! No!" She dropped from the hammock. The big kitten playfully leaped upon her and rolled her to the floor. She fought him off and struggled to her feet and at long last sobbed for all things lost.

She cried for the pa-hay-okee.

She cried for the big trees.

She cried for the Calusa Indians, the ibis, the orchids, the panthers and egrets . . . the voiceless members of the Earth Clan.

And she cried for the broken bowl.

When all her tears had flowed, she went ashore, picked bulrushes and grass and returned home to weave a basket for the broken pieces. She worked quietly.

Coootchobee sensed his mother's change of mood and came across the floor. He sat down in front of her, black nose and mask like smudges on his face. His large eyes focused on her. The pupils dilated in anxiety.

"You are too curious for your own good," she said sternly. "Perhaps you should be on punishment, too. A dunking? A spanking? Or leaving you here to starve to death?" The sunlight fell on the young panther's healthy fur, turning him into a bright golden object.

"That would be sinful," she said. "There are only a few of you left on Earth. And you do good work. You keep life balanced in the swamp." She reached out and rubbed his twisting ears. "There are other fingers to make bowls, but only you can make coootchobees." The panther purred, rubbed his head against hers and stretched out on his side. His whiskers moved like steel antennae, picking up messages from the wilderness.

Billie Wind wondered how she would cook her food now; on a spit? in the coals? Her eyes fell on the iron teapot.

"You," she said to the pot. "And you will not break."

That night she lay in her hammock looking up at the stars and wondering if they were part of the Earth, too.

"Who is out there?" she asked. "Who are the people of the stars; and do they war and fight other people of the stars like the movies say they do? Do they have alligators and panthers? Do they have swamps and tree islands? Do they have beautiful birds?"

A Florida yellow bat flew out of the forest and tumbled in front of the stars.

"Can you answer that, bat? Or this? Can you answer this? Do the planets that spin around the distant suns have yellow bats like you?

"And finally, are there really living things out there? I wonder." She rolled over and looked down. Coootcho-bee was awake, staring into the darkness. She wished he would speak, for at that moment she felt he knew the truth about the animal gods, the serpents, the dwarfs—and the planets of the stars.

"Tell me, Coootchobee," she whispered. The panther turned his head and looked up at her. His night-seeing eyes were wise and perceptive.

The houseboat moved only a few miles each day as Billie Wind labored it toward the sea. To keep track of their progress she drew her course, as she figured it, on the floor of the houseboat with a piece of charcoal.

"It seems we have wound almost back to where we started from," she said to Coootchobee one day. He had learned to climb the posts and get into her hammock, and this morning his big hind feet were flailing above her head as he swung back and forth. He looked up, discovered the orchids hanging from the roof and swatted them. His claws stuck in the thatching and, as the hammock swung inward, he clung to the roof, grabbed with the other paw and clambered atop.

"NO, Coootchobee," Billie Wind admonished, shaking her finger at the kitten. Petang, who was sleeping in the crate, awoke at the commotion and peered up at the tail of the panther dangling above him.

A large hind foot came through the roof, then another and a rear end. Petang dove into the water. Billie Wind shinnied up the post, grabbed the kitten by the tail and pulled. He meowed, spat and dug in his claws. She yanked until she could grip one hind foot. Palm fronds fell to the floor, then Billie Wind, kitten and bamboo slats came down with a crash. The spitting angry Coootchobee was in her lap. Before she could push him off, he rolled her as if she were another kitten. His claws dug into her flesh. She screamed, twisted free and picked up a stick. Coootchobee stopped playing and sat down.

"You *are* a handful, Coootchobee," she said, lowering the weapon and catching a sailing feather from her shirt. She examined her scratches, then washed them with water. Docking the boat she walked into the grass and picked the leaves of a plant called poor man's patches, which she pasted on her wounds. They stuck like Band-Aids and stopped the bleeding, for they have fuzzy spikes on the underside that adhere to almost everything. Early settlers mended rents in clothing and Indians patched flesh scratches with the plant leaves. With her wounds attended to, she gathered several palm leaves, climbed to the roof of the houseboat and repaired the damage.

Late in the afternoon of the following day she shoved off from the shore and poled down the quiet Fahkahatchee Slough. To the west a flock of vultures soared above the trees at the water's edge. "I know what you are saying," she called to the birds as they spiraled down to earth. "Some dead creature lies below you. That's what you are saying." The birds circled lower on their giant six-foot wings. Just when she expected them to alight, they tensed, flapped their wings and climbed into the sky.

Billie Wind leaned on her pole.

"Why don't you fly down and eat?" she asked.

The birds soared higher and higher, circling far above the land.

"You see an enemy, don't you?" she said to the birds. "You are afraid." She picked up the pole to push on, then thought better of it. Perhaps the dead animal was a deer. Coootchobee was eating so much now that a deer would be welcome. She hesitated, remembering an enemy was evidently at the carcass, maybe a bear. Whatever it was it would run at her approach, she presumed. She picked up her machete, slipped into the water and waded toward shore.

The birds circled lower as she approached. That said to Billie Wind that possibly the enemy had smelled her and run off.

Crouching slightly, she pushed through a barrier of alligator flags and came ashore on all fours, her eyes on the vultures. Their circling now told her that the animal was to the left and deeper into the forest. Without crackling a leaf she walked to the left and peered around a palmetto onto a grassy meadow.

An adult male panther and a cub were feeding on the carcass of a deer. Billie Wind held her breath. The adult was a glorious animal. His eyes were soft, his muscles strong beneath his shiny fur. The cub was about the age of Coootchobee.

The male turned his head to the side and with two powerful slashes of his teeth severed off a leg of the prey and carried it to the base of a palm. He dug into the ground and buried it. The cub finished eating a morsel and lay down in the sun, her sides bulging with food. She yawned and batted a butterfly. Male panthers rarely help raise the young, but Three-Hands-on-the-Saddle told tales of several that did. Apparently this panther was one of those.

Upon returning to the carcass, the male lifted his head and froze. The kitten sensed his concern and lowered her head. Something was amiss, Billie Wind read. Did the panther know she was there? Would he attack? She looked for the nearest tree. The first branch was twenty feet up. It was best to sit still as the rabbits do when a hawk flies over. If she did not move she might not be seen. That's how animal prey survive. Nevertheless, she wanted to run, knowing full well that would be the worst thing she could do. Running away inspires predators to get up and give chase. Using all her willpower she quieted her breathing and sat motionless.

The male panther focused his eyes in her direction.

His great nostrils flared as they sucked in the scents on the wind.

Merrow, he snarled; he turned and with one movement leaped ten feet into the forest. He vanished among the palmettos. The kitten sniffed the air to see what had alarmed her father and followed him at a run. The *merrow,* Billie Wind now knew, meant: "flee." Although the panthers were out of sight she did not move; instead she watched the vultures. From their vantage point high in the sky they kept their eyes on the panthers. For a long while they circled high above the trees, then at last spiraled down on the carcass.

That was her signal. She got to her feet and ran to the kill, took the animal by a foot and as the vultures flew up, dragged it to the water. She floated the bloated carcass to the boat where both Petang and Coootchobee were wide awake, standing on the edge watching her. When Billie Wind heaved the deer aboard, it slipped back; they pounced on it, then pulled and tugged until it was secure in the middle of the boat.

Coootchobee sniffed the message "panther" on the carcass. He screeched like an alley cat. Billie Wind and Petang stepped back, not knowing what he was announcing. When he finally quieted down Billie Wind took her machete and dressed out the fresh venison.

While she was cutting the tenderloin, Coootchobee suddenly arose and charged to the edge of the boat. He howled mournfully, then wailed out a scream that hurt Billie Wind's ears. Prickles of fear ran up her spine. Petang crawled into her lap.

The reeds parted and the male panther strode toward them. He held his head high like an Indian chief. Then he gathered his legs under him to spring.

Merrrrrr, purred Coootchobee and dropped to his belly. The old panther's head glowed in the sun, and all fear died within Billie Wind. She marveled at her calmness. The old legends *were* true; the panther inspired peace before death. Billie Wind sat quietly, her hands folded in her lap, unafraid to die.

As the panther crouched she heard him purr. That seemed strange. Purring was a sound of love, not death. But before she could wonder any more he had leaped onto the boat and was looking at Billie Wind. She did not move.

He blinked, lowered his gaze and took a grip on Coootchobee's neck. He picked him up. The kitten curled his head into his groin. His hind feet arose to meet his chin.

The panther leaped out over the water holding Coootchobee in his mouth. He floated like a spear, straight and silent. Landing with a splash, he bounded into the forest, reminiscent of water and wind, and was gone.

For a long time Billie Wind stared into the parted grasses where Coootchobee and his father had vanished. The vultures circled the boat, a breeze blew a cloud of mosquitoes past and Billie Wind arose and picked up her pole.

"Good-bye, Coootchobee," she whispered. "Good-bye. Live well and long and fill the Everglades with your children and your children's children." She dropped her head, for she loved Coootchobee.

Petang sighed with relief, for he did not. Billie Wind laughed, put down her pole and gathered him into her arms.

"You have always been my first love," she said.

The little otter would not be mothered long for he, too, was growing up. He wiggled from her arms, sniffed the deer meat and helped himself to a morsel. While he ate, Billie Wind built a fire and filled her teapot with venison. She placed it on the rock stove and picked up her pole.

"We are not getting anywhere very fast," she said, and poled harder, determined to labor until the stars came out and the venison was done. It was very late when she sat cross-legged on the floor beside Petang and ate her dinner. A new moon came up, reminding her how long she had been gone. She thought of Mamau Whispering Wind, and of Mary and Charlie Wind. She thought of her father and her brother.

The Mute One

For the next weeks the houseboat moved through quiet places. It passed strands of gray-green trees and wound through miles of sparkling saw grass prairie. It slid over water lilies and blooming bladderworts. And each day the sun rose through the mist, quickly dried the moisture from the air then blazed across the sky to set in serpent colors—red, orange and yellow.

Butterflies rested on the houseboat. Spiders took up residence in the corners under the roof. A kingbird rode on the top of the thatch for almost two hours. He flew out, darted through the sky catching insects and came back. When the boat had traveled almost a mile he stayed behind to chase a crow almost five times his size.

Billie Wind thought about the kingbird hunting the sky.

"We all fit together," she mused. "The kingbirds in the sky, the spiders in the corners, the otters in the water and the panthers in the night forest.

"And me?

"Where do I fit?" She studied her hands and feet. "In all places; in the sky, in the corners, in the water, in the forest, even in space. Human beings fit anywhere. We can make ourselves comfortable in ice and sun, on the sea and on the land. But the birds and spiders and fish and otters and panthers can not. So will they pass away as we change the Earth?" She watched a dragonfly come aboard to rest and scan the sky for mosquitoes. An egret alighted on the roof and preened his feathers for flight. A frog jumped aboard.

And each found its spot in accordance with its needs.

Now that the drought was broken, rain fell every afternoon on schedule. It filled the slough, the cypress swamps, the saw grass prairie. Water shimmered from horizon to horizon beneath trees and grass blades. Life multiplied and filled the air and waters and forests.

The temperature stayed high in the nineties. Flies bit and laid eggs at the precise moment when the humidity reached ninety-nine percent and before it reached one hundred percent and rained. Billie Wind swatted the insects and finally smeared her bare skin with fish oil. She slept in the heat of the day and poled in the coolness of the rain and the night. With each rain the river rose higher and the houseboat moved seaward more easily.

One morning Billie Wind rolled out of her hammock to note that the water had changed. It was crystal clear and free of lilies and bladderworts. There were fewer weeds and more fish. She leaned over the edge of the boat. Petang was already in swimming, excitedly chasing the abundant fish. He darted past the boat chasing a school of large fish underwater. With a swish of his short legs and webbed toes he plunged, then surfaced with one in his mouth. Billie Wind put the ramp in the water and he came aboard. The fish was unusual, and she stuck her fingers in its gills and pulled it from Petang's mouth. He shook water all over her face and arms in thanks.

"It's a snook," she said, noting its yellowish pointed nose. "What's it doing here?" She glanced from the fish to the trees. They had changed from cypress to black mangroves, trees of the coast. Each tree had many little knees coming up from its roots.

"The snook is talking to me, Petang," she said. "But again I can't hear. What is he saying?" She gave the fish back to the otter, who snatched it energetically and carried it to the far side of his crate.

"All right, don't answer me," she said as he devoured the fish, his stiff whiskers twitching with the ecstasy of filling his stomach. By the time he had finished his meal, the water on Billie Wind's arms and face had dried, leaving white spots. She tasted one with the tip of her tongue.

"Petang," she exclaimed. "You did answer me. You talked in your splashes. They are salty. We have reached brackish water. The sea is not far."

She pushed the houseboat to shore and tied it to a stout limb.

"We have a problem, Petang," she said. Sleepy now, he was retired in his crate, stretched out on his back, his paws folded on his chest, his webbed toes relaxed.

"How will we get fresh water in the mangrove swamp? We may be wandering around in the islands and tree corridors for days and years. We'll need fresh water." Petang closed his eyes.

"I know," she went on aloud. "We'll drink rain. That's fresh. But how do I catch it and how do I store it?"

A thought occurred to her. She untied the boat and poled it back upstream. She had seen a short, stout log on the buttonwood levee. The buttonwood trees grew on a high land built by the waves and tidal waters over the ages forming a natural dam between the fresh water of the pa-hay-okee and the salty water of the mangroves.

Many miles back she found the log, shoved it aboard and promptly went to work chipping out its center to form a bowl that would hold water. Petang awoke, sniffed her work with his blunt nose and rolled to all fours. He yawned as he walked to the ramp. Sliding down it into the water he swam ashore and disappeared in a grove of bamboo trees.

"That gives me an idea," she said and picked up her

machete. She followed Petang into the grove, where she cut down several of the bigger trees and trimmed off their branches. One she split in half, chipped out the nodes between the hollows and stepped back to look at her rainspout. Toting all aboard the houseboat, she tied the spout to the roof with vines tilting at an angle, so that the rainwater running off the thatch would flow downward into her hollowed log.

When the water catcher was finished and installed, Billie Wind stayed on the levee for a few more days gathering plants. She filled a basket with soapberries, palmetto seeds and the fruits of the cocoplums. She would not be able to harvest any of these once she had entered the salt water, for they required fresh water. She knew she might find other tasty herbs like saltwort along the coast, but she might not, too. A plant in the hand was worth two on the beach.

As she was untying the houseboat after all her preparations for the coastal islands were made, she whistled for Petang. He answered from the middle of the bamboo grove.

"Come on," she called. "Time to leave." Petang dashed out of the foliage, dove into the water, rolled over and over and sped back up the bank to the grove. He snorted.

"Oh, all right," she shouted. "I'll come see what you've got." Running down the ramp she pushed through the brush to an open glade in the midst of the bamboos. Petang was leaping and buckling like a whip around a frightened gopher turtle. She was about a foot long and six inches high and was marked prettily with tan and brown diamonds and squares.

"Hello, turtle," she said. "You look like a Seminole garment. I'll bet the ancient women got their inspiration for their intricate designs from you." She glanced at Petang. What did he want her to do? Bring the turtle along? Shrugging her shoulders she picked up the silent reptile and held her in front of her face. She studied the somber eyes and blunt nose.

"I think you have something to say to me," she said. "All the other animals have, but since you are mute and expressionless I guess it will take you a long time to say it. Come along. You can ride with us until I can hear you." She turned to Petang. "Let's go."

With the turtle tucked under her arm she returned to the houseboat and made haste to depart. When she put the big turtle down, she promptly crawled under the mats in the manner of her kind, the gopher turtles, who burrow and dwell underground in the dark and coolness.

"I am going to name you Burden, little lady turtle," she said. "And I'll tell you why. There is an old Indian legend that says the Earth rests on the back of the quiet turtle, who carries all our troubles and woes."

When Petang came aboard and had settled down in his crate, Billie Wind wondered if he had wanted her to do just what she had done: bring the turtle aboard the boat. He had seemed to tell her that, for he had not dragged or bitten Burden.

"No," she said, "that's ridiculous." He had simply

snorted at a turtle and she had picked her up because she liked her drooping eyes and snub nose.

Billie Wind clambered up on the crate, put her pole in the water and, as she leaned on it, saw that an afternoon thunderstorm was gathering. She steered out into the middle of the channel to keep an eager eye on the storm.

Within a few moments the clouds dumped rain in great silver streaks, the rain ran down the palm leaves into the rainspout and downhill into her wooden vessel. Several inches collected before the storm blew on. She scooped up a conchful, sipped and passed the cup to Petang.

"Have a drink of our own water," she said. He stuck his nose in, blew and showered it in all directions.

"You'll not be so reckless when we get to the salt water," she said and took another long drink before climbing back on the crate. Sitting cross-legged, she used the paddle as a rudder and steered the houseboat in the current.

The houseboat slid down the Fahkahatchee Slough.

It floated past the buttonwood levee, over the shallows and into the black mangrove swamp. A dark water mark on the tree trunks and rushes told Billie Wind she was back in tidewater.

"Now I must think of tides and pulls and pushes," she said.

Burden, the turtle, plodded out from under the mats and stretched out her wrinkled neck.

"Tides and pulls and pushes," Billie Wind repeated

so loudly the turtle pulled her head back into her shell. Billie Wind stood up on the crate and peered over the roof. She cupped her hand behind her ear listening to a *ka-swoosh a-swoosh*.

"Automobiles," she said nervously. "Highway 41."

Dragging the paddle like a brake, she slowed the houseboat down.

"How will I get over the road?" Dams and gates blocked the rivers and canals near the Big Cypress Indian Reservation, and she remembered her father and uncle portaging the heavy dugouts around them. She could not possibly lift her houseboat. She might have to dismantle it, or abandon it. Both choices were dangerous. She had a mission to complete and friends to take care of.

"I don't want to be found now," she said. "I've gone too far and am too close to the answer I seek.

"The animals talk. That I do know. What I don't know is what they are saying . . . all of them together, I mean. They are crying something, and I can not make it out.

"The mute turtle knows. But I cannot hear her. Not because she is mute. That does not matter. Birds talk with their flights, Petang talks with his deeds and so the turtle will talk to me somehow.

"And when I hear what she has to say, it will be time for me to go home.

"But not now, Highway 41." She shook her fist and poled the houseboat under the drooping limbs of some willows, tied up and jumped into the shallow water. Moving quietly she waded to the next bend in the river and peered around it. The slough flowed under a bridge. There were no dams or gates. She sighed.

Pleased that something was working out for her, she returned to her houseboat and lay down by the hearth until the stars came out and the owls flew off toward the pine forests. She arose and, in the darkness, poled the houseboat under the bridge and the rumble of traffic and out into the red mangrove swamps that border the Gulf of Mexico. Somewhere in the open water she laid down her pole, checked the sleeping Petang and the wide-awake Burden, then climbed into her hammock and slept.

She awoke under an arch of red mangroves. The sun lit the water, sending ripples of light running on the undersides of the dark oval leaves. She sat up. Several egrets and herons stalked the shallows under the root arches. Shrimp larvae darted in jerks and spurts through the water. Beady-eyed fish swam by. The mangrove swamps are nurseries for many of the sea creatures, and they darkened the water with their whirling masses.

Petang came loping under the arches toward the boat. As he was about to come aboard, a sea bass fry caught his attention and he plunged after it. Billie Wind rubbed her eyes and studied the roots of a mangrove.

"Oysters," she exclaimed. "Mangrove oysters." Picking up a basket she slid down the ramp and gathered as many as she could find.

Petang came up the ramp as she came home, carrying a fish in his mouth.

"I don't know where we are," she said. "But we are

getting close to something." She tossed a plastic bottle and a beer can on the deck.

She cooked her freshwater vegetables and oysters, then climbed up on her roof to get her bearings. All around stretched the shiny dark mangroves. They arched darkly over channels, hid bird rookeries, made islands and island chains. Then she noticed that the boat was drifting into the setting sun.

"I think the Ten Thousand Islands and the Indian villages are more southerly," she mused. "But the tide is pulling us west. How can I fight the tide? I don't want to go west."

As she took up the pole her eyes fell on the mats she had woven.

"Sails," she said. "I'll make a sail to catch the wind. If I angle it just right it should work."

From one of the bamboo sticks she hung a neatly fashioned mat, then ran a stout bamboo pole up the middle and fastened the mat along it. This she carried to the bow and set it up so that the offshore wind struck it. The pole strained, the mat held the wind and the houseboat quickened its pace. Billie Wind guided it using her paddle as a rudder.

"We are going south," she observed, "but not westerly enough now." She made another sail and rigged it at a different angle and ran back to her paddle. She steered toward the southwest.

The houseboat looked more like a county fair than a vessel, with its sails flopping, animals tucked under eaves and in crates, and flowers swinging from the roof. It slipped by dark mangrove islands where ibis fed their young and eventually into a wide, turquoise-blue bay.

Slowly, ploddingly, it made progress with the wind behind it, even against the outgoing tide, which is not very strong in the Ten Thousand Islands, rising and falling a foot at the most.

It passed close to an egret island. One of the long-legged, long-necked birds cast an eye at the craft of palm leaves, smoke, rainspouts and reed sails, as it blew past her in the wind. The bird blinked and turned away. Billie Wind and her houseboat were not of the egret's world. They were neither food, nor nest, nor danger, and so they vanished from the bird's sight as if they had not been there at all.

The next day when the sun was overhead and too hot for any sensible creature to move about, Burden came out from under the last remaining mat and helped herself to coconut meat. She chewed slowly, her drooping eyes speaking to Billie Wind of lost seas and primitive lands. Her curled mouth line seemed to say that living inside a bony house had its advantages and was pleasurable. When she had eaten she thumped back under the mat.

"Now what kind of a message was that?" Billie Wind asked the turtle.

A thunderstorm billowed up in the late afternoon and the winds stiffened. Billie Wind had to change the sails to catch this energy head on. The houseboat swayed, then leaped forward, and she leaned heavily on the paddle to steer a straight course down the middle of the turquoise bay.

From the rooftop she could see a wide channel lined with islands that seemed to be leading somewhere. She steered into this corridor, watching the shore for signs of people.

"Oil and Styrofoam," she said to Petang and Burden. "We are getting close to something."

She tied up at night and sailed by day, stopping on the islands now and then to gather coconuts and firewood. Days and nights passed and still there was no sign of a village or people.

One evening she reached into the water and pulled up a mat made of sabal palms. "Seminole," she cried. "Petang, we are close to our people." She slept lightly that night, wondering which clan it would be and if the people might have some information about Panther Paw.

At dawn she put up the sails, poled into the wind and rode a snappy breeze around one island and into the mouth of another river. On a spit of white sand grew an avocado and an orange tree. Her heart pounded as she climbed to her roof to see who was there. She saw no one, no houses, no boats.

"A deserted fishing camp," she said and, adjusting her sails, wended her way across the blue water toward the beach, wondering who had made their camp there. Fishermen? Tourists? Shell hunters? As she drew close she saw the red flowers of a morning glory with large roots that tasted like sweet potato.

"Seminoles!" she exclaimed, recognizing the flowers of the plants that the Indian hunters and fishermen planted wherever they camped along the coast.

After taking down the sails she poled the houseboat into a cove near the beach. Then she jumped ashore and ran to the water's edge. The waves were green, the water crystal clear. She took off her feather shirt, her trousers and shoes and dove into the water, rolling and turning, happy to know that she had found a place frequented by her own people.

"Maybe they will come here tomorrow, or the next day."

Holding her nose she went under the water to see who lived in that world. Petang shot past in a silver bubble of air. She grinned as he turned, came back and sped under her arm. She chased him a short distance; then they both surfaced and swam ashore.

She tossed him a shell. He tumbled over and over with it, batted it into the air and suddenly stood on his big hind feet. His eyes were focused on the meadow behind the beach, his ears twitched. Billie threw him another shell. He ignored it.

"Come on. Let's play," she said. "I'm stiff from sitting." But Petang did not look her way. Dropping to all fours he flowed like water across the sand and vanished into the beach grasses.

"Who's there?" she called. "What do you see?" For a moment she felt a chill of fear in her veins, then a Cape Sable sparrow sang and told her that no person was there. She relaxed. Petang's head popped up, then down. She waited, but he did not appear again.

She turned her attention to food. A coconut palm near the houseboat bore a cluster of nuts, but it was too straight to climb with her hands and feet. Picking up a coconut husk, she shredded its fibers and braided them into a rope. This she threw around the tree and, taking the ends in her hands, flipped it higher than her head. She leaned back on it, put her feet on the trunk and walked up and after flipping it a few more times, gained the top and threw down several green and several ripe coconuts. Then she descended on her flip rope.

Fresh coconut milk was such a treat that she drank two nutsful of the sweet, waterlike beverage and was opening a third when a brown pelican flew over the beach. He splashed down onto the water, folded his huge wings to his side and paddled boldly toward her.

"You're not afraid of people, are you? I know what that means. Fishermen feed you fish guts and you've lost all fear of man.

"It also means I am not far from a village." The bird stared at the remains of one of Petang's fish on the ramp. Billie Wind got up and threw it to him and watched him flap across the water on his enormous wings, lunge, fill his beak and pouch with fish and water and swallow.

"That's a bribe. Which way is the village?" He turned a coy eye upon her. "Fly to the village and show me the way." The bird circled on the water with his webbed feet, then steamed like a tugboat toward the ramp. There he waited for more.

Petang came rippling out of the grasses, rubbed his neck on the sand, rolled over, turned a loop-de-loop and ran back where he had come from. Billie Wind scratched her chin.

"What is the matter with you, Petang? Have you sipped the black drink?"

The bending grasses marked Petang's travels through the meadow and straight toward the trees. Then Billie Wind saw, coming from the forest, another ripple of grass. It met Petang's and threaded alongside to the reeds at the water's edge. There were two otters.

"Petang, don't leave me. Not yet." He snorted and sprang out of the grasses down the beach and into the water in graceful leaps. He loped up the ramp to the houseboat and looked out at his friend. She did not follow. Flopping to his belly, he slid into the water and came up in the reeds. He ran off with his bright-eyed friend.

"Petang's in love," she murmured and felt a knot rise in her throat. It was not the breeding season of the otters, but they often ran with future mates in the late summer and fall. It saddened her to think that Petang might not be with her much longer. "Unless, unless I can make a pet of his friend.

"I'll stay here until I tame her," she resolved and went to the boat for her fishnet.

The pelican floated alongside the boat waiting for another handout. After some time, he gave up and, flapping his three-foot wings and drawing back his head, ran on the water until he got airborne. Then he skimmed over the waves with strong beats and soared over the trees on the other side of the channel.

Billie Wind ran to the stern of the boat to see where he was going, but he was gone before she could get a good view.

"Is that the way to the village?" she called.

The reeds thrashed where the otters played, the grasses bent under their footsteps and Billie Wind watched as they returned to the forest.

"Petang, come back," she called.

But he did not come back, although she caught a large snook and laid it by his crate.

She lit a fire and ate by herself. When the stars came out she stretched out on the warm beach and wondered if she should give up her quest. She would never hear what the animals had to say. She did not even understand Petang, and she knew him well.

"I have no answer for Charlie Wind. Just observations on their lives. And he won't like that. Too practical."

Plunk, plunk, plunk. Burden the turtle was walking across the floor of the houseboat tapping out sounds which seemed to say something. *Plunk.* She sat up and listened. The waves lapped softly on the sand; the tree frogs sang. Burden was silent.

"Is that all you have to say, old turtle?"

Clutching her knees she pulled them up to her chin and stared up at her star. "Petang has not come home," she said. "I wish he would."

For many days Billie Wind enjoyed the beach and water. She gathered saltwort, braided husks into rope and watched the meadow for Petang and his friend. There was no sign of them. Only the sparrow flitted among the grasses.

One morning as she dragged her net through the water on her way to set it, there was a swirl at her feet and Petang popped up.

"Little otter," she cried joyously. "I'm so glad you're back." She reached out; he dove between her hands and caught one of the little fish nibbling her toes. He snorted and buckled ashore and before she could join him he was in the meadow running gracefully toward his rendezvous in the forest.

The next morning when the tide was out, Billie Wind wandered among the low spots in the reeds, tracking the otters' footsteps. Their webbed prints were plainly visible in the mud, but disappeared on the high dry land and she could not follow them. Thoughtfully she returned to her boat.

Plunk, plunk, plunk. Billie Wind walked slowly up the ramp and sat down beside the turtle. She put her elbows on her knees and her chin in her hands. Her eyes scanned the water and sky. A cloud, an odd-looking thing, as thin and gray as a spider's web, was moving clockwise across the sun. She studied it a long time trying to make sense of it, for it seemed full of meaning.

She brushed her hair and pondered the cloud. The water below the stern of the houseboat gurgled and swirled into whirlpools. Billie Wind shinnied up a roof support to get a better view. Under the water moved a huge blimplike body, with a small head and two flippers. The animal swam this way and that as if looking for something.

"A manatee, a sea cow!"

Billie Wind jumped to the floor, picked up a short piece of hollow bamboo and put it in her mouth for a snorkle. She eased into the water without making a ripple, went under and paddled toward the gentle mammal of the warm coastal waters of North and South America. These peaceable sirens once lived in great numbers, feeding on the weeds in rivers and estuaries, but rapidly died out with the coming of the motorboat. High-speed propellers slashed and wounded the sirens until only a rare few still exist.

Billie Wind had never seen one. She took a breath and dove deep. The manatee was one of the animal gods, and she approached it reverently. She noted its wrinkled gray skin and whalelike tail. It had a triangular mouth and a split lip that could pick weeds like fingers. Around the mouth was a muff of sensitive whiskers, walruslike, Billie Wind thought.

Through the clear water Billie Wind could see a baby floundering. If this was what the mother was looking for, she was looking the wrong way, for she was coming toward Billie. The sea cow moved close and touched her with a flipper.

"I'm not your baby," Billie Wind thought as the manatee coddled her. Suddenly the animal saw her with a beady eye, turned and with the other eye saw her baby. Pumping her tail up and down the mother reached the calf, picked it up on her flipper and moved toward the open sea. Billie Wind surfaced.

"Why are you going to sea? The mouth of the river is the other way. The deep weedless water is no place for a manatee." Billie Wind glanced up at the sky. The slender twisting cloud had become many clouds strung out in an enormous arc.

The manatees came up for a breath of air and went under. Their trail to the open water was marked by ripples.

"Are you wounded?" she wondered. "Or do you know something I don't know?"

Back aboard the houseboat she dipped up enough rainwater into her pot to cover a large morning glory tuber and placed it on her fire. She swept the floor. She studied the sky and then went to the beach to fish.

The sand crabs were burrowing deep into the sand. She shrugged and waded into the water.

The clouds thickened. Late in the afternoon she wandered out into the meadow to look for Petang and his friend. There were no footprints in the mud at the base of the reeds.

"They're gone," she said. "How can they fish in the forest? Why have they left the water?" She turned slowly, studying the softly swaying trees, the dipping blades of grass.

"What do they know that I don't know?" She walked into the bushes tapping them with a stick.

"The sparrow is gone."

Plunk, plunk, plunk. The turtle was talking as she walked up the ramp. Burden reached the edge of the houseboat and stretched her neck out until almost all the wrinkles were gone, then she dug with one foot and stopped. *Plunk.*

"I'm listening," said Billie Wind. "I'm listening."
Plunk.

After a fried-fish supper Billie Wind stretched out in her hammock and waited for the birds to come back to the roosts in the mangroves that bordered the channel to the north. Only a few returned, and she wondered about that. A flock of willets flew inland in the dusk.

"Everyone is going somewhere," she said. "Is there a fire?"

Then she sensed the flight of the animals had something to do with the strange, twisting clouds. The air was heavy and difficult to breathe. She walked to the stern of the houseboat and leaned on a roof support to observe the wild things. Out of the gloom came a family of spoonbills, beautiful pink birds with long necks and legs. Their spoon-shaped beaks filter minute plants and animals from the inland ponds. They too were on their way. They saw the thatched roof of the houseboat, circled and dropped down to rest. Billie Wind moved to see them better and they spread their wings and flew on.

During the night she awoke and searched the meadow once more for Petang. "He's grown up," she said as she climbed the plank. "I must get used to that."

Plunk, plunk, plunk. Burden almost walked off the boat into the water. Billie Wind grabbed her, for it would have been a fatal plunge. She was a land turtle.

"Tell me, everyone. Tell me, what is happening!"

The wind gusted fitfully. Billie Wind sat down on the floor and stroked the turtle's humped back.

"The birds are flying inland, the manatee is headed into the deep waters of the Gulf, the sand crabs are digging into the sand and the spoonbills are behaving strangely. What does it all mean?"

She crawled into her hammock. "Sometimes I wish we lived in more innocent times when the animals really did talk to people."

In the morning she pulled up a net full of fish. The tide was far out, farther than she had ever seen it; and it was still going.

"Now I know," she said, watching the foreboding tide. "A bad storm is coming. A really bad storm.

"A hurricane."

Billie Wind had only heard tales of the devastating

hurricanes that had pounded the Florida coast in the past. Mamau Whispering Wind had told her how the winds and tides had turned buildings to sticks and washed away railroads, bridges and entire towns. Billie Wind had never lived through a hurricane, for almost her entire life had been spent in the drought years; and so hurricanes were only vivid tales to her. And one of these tales was how far out the tide went before it came thundering in.

In the morning she prepared for departure. She would join the otters and birds and go inland to safety. She cooked the fish and a batch of morning glory tubers; gathered coconuts and whacked the meat from them. She wrapped them all in grass and stored them in Mamau Whispering Wind's deerskin pouch. Then she picked up her machete.

She cut the vines that held the thatch in place. She took down the sails, the rainspout, the roof and the masts. She unlashed the boards of the floor and removed them. She slashed the log from the dugout and pushed it out into the mud. She could go faster in the dugout than in the awkward houseboat. The crate she decided to leave behind. She took her tools and pot and the fresh-water vessel. She tied a coconut rope around the waist of her bird-skin shirt and braided her hair.

She was ready to go inland. As she picked up Burden, who was digging into the sand, she heard the wind roar like colliding freight trains. In the ensuing silence she covered Burden and her possessions with her mats, climbed into the bow and pushed off. The tide was now quite high. It picked her up and swept her into the middle of the channel.

She watched the meadow until she was around the bend and it was out of sight.

"Petang," she called. "Live well and long."

Plunk.

Oats

Burden at her feet, her leggings tucked in her boots, Billie Wind paddled toward the mouth of the river on the incoming tide. She followed the route the spoonbills had taken. Occasionally she glanced back. The clouds were drab sponges, heavy with water, pocked and gray. Her ears ached as the atmospheric pressure dropped lower and lower.

"That's what the animals heard," she said, shaking her head. "The voice of the low."

Three white herons flew overhead, their wings bowing deeply in a strenuous effort to keep aloft in the humid air.

"Mamau Whispering Wind," Billie Wind murmured as the birds of good fortune flew over. "You gave me a strong back. It is better than a charm. But you also gave me a practical mind and I am going to follow the path of the white herons. They are flying to safety."

The birds soared over an island and dropped out of sight. Billie Wind paddled harder, skimming along the edge of the island and into a corridor overhung with mangroves. A violet-blue bay gleamed at the end. She could see the white herons. They were resting on a stump beyond the corridor.

Protected by the trees from the gusting winds, she rode the speeding water down the tunnel. A wrecked sailboat was jammed among some tree trunks. She wished she had time to stop and search it for useful articles. A sail caught her eye. She backwatered and came alongside the boat.

Lifting up a broken mast, she tugged loose a small nylon sail and stuffed it under the mats. Quickly she climbed back into the bow and paddled hard to make up for lost time.

The tide had almost stopped running out. She had about an hour before it turned and started galloping in with such force that she would not be able to withstand it.

"Thirteen feet," she said. "I must get thirteen feet above sea level to be safe from the tidal wave." She recalled the warnings posted in the Florida schools and public places.

The white herons unfolded their wings, flapped them

and glided out over the bay. She dug in her paddle and followed. Sliding out of the corridor she saw that the bay was really the wide mouth of a river. The herons crossed the ruffled surface and dropped onto a beach. After a moment they took to their wings again and flew up the river. She stood up. Far ahead of them the land bulged distinctly.

"High land." She sat down. "Could that be the village?"

If so she would have to cross the choppy bay to get to it. If the tide turned when she was in the middle she might be swept away. She thought she had better cling to the shore. But it was miles and miles around. Should she chance it and follow the birds across the bay?

She decided to follow the birds. The bay was growing quieter. The gusts had stopped and the tide had not turned. Lifting her paddle, getting down on her knees, she plunged the dugout onto the steely water. Swiftly she slipped across the surface.

Out of the corner of her eyes she watched the twigs and leaves on the water. Gratefully, she saw they were not moving, going neither inland nor out to sea. They were standing still waiting ominously for the change. She lowered her head and stroked harder. Burden looked up, then pulled her head inside her shell.

The leaves started out to sea. At first they barely moved, but as the storm drew the bay water into its center of low pressure, they began to move faster and faster. Faster and faster. Billie Wind shouted as she fought the tide.

The dugout moved slower and slower. Then it stopped. She paddled forward furiously. It slipped and moved backward.

She was only one hundred feet from the beach where the herons had been. She glanced behind her in terror. A straight path led to the sea.

Her eyes fell on the upturned stump of a tree. She steered toward it with one hand while pulling out the sail with the other. As she came alongside she threw the sail over the roots. The snags caught it and she held on. The dugout slowed down and came to a stop.

The tide ran on seaward.

Now what to do?

In five hours the tide would turn again and start back. Could she hang on that long? And if she could, would the storm and the tidal wave come with it? She wrapped the sail around her wrists and held on tighter. She counted. She sang. She listed the herbs in the black drink. She thought of Mamau Whispering Wind and of Charlie Wind. What would they do? Never mind what Charlie Wind would do, what would Whispering Wind do? She took off her headband and tied her wrists to the sail. She tensed her thigh muscles to hold the boat beneath her.

Then the sail went slack. She was no longer straining. She looked over the gunnel. The dugout was grounded on the bottom of the bay. She was high, dry and safe.

Slowly she got to her feet, untied her wrists and studied her situation. She was far from the trickle of water that was the river, but close to the beach. She must abandon her boat and walk. Slinging her deerskin pouch on her back, she picked up the fish spear and tucked the sail into her belt. She took a long drink of fresh water and picked up Burden.

Billie Wind eased out of the dugout, testing the depth of the mire. It was only a few inches deep. Beneath the black residue from the swamp was firm sand. She walked swiftly, not even turning around to bid her dugout good-bye.

Safely on the beach she dropped her possessions, promptly climbed a tree and searched the landscape for the white herons. There was no sign of them; but north along the river was a mound covered with fig and palm trees.

"Calusa mound!" She slid to the ground. "Let's go, Burden." She picked up the turtle, who was digging into the ground again.

Billie Wind recounted the little she knew about the mysterious Calusa. "They understood hurricanes," she said to herself. "They built their villages on stilts above the tidal waves. They constructed forty-foot-high shell mounds on which, some people said, their chiefs lived. That makes sense. From such heights they could see enemies, ships; plan strategies; and, above all, avoid the deadly hurricanes."

Lining up three trees with the mound she walked from one to the next, keeping herself on a beeline course with her destination. Once she climbed a tree and looked back.

The bay was empty. The bottom gleamed like quicksilver in the eerie light.

"In five hours it will all come raging back." Shifting Burden to her other arm, she lined up three more trees and plunged into a red mangrove swamp, the worst walking in the world.

The looping roots and interlocking limbs slowed her down to a turtle's pace, for she was forced to climb over some and wedge herself under others. Occasionally she took out her machete and slashed through the binding meshes. She slipped in the mire, fell, got up and walked on.

Two hours later the mosquitoes stopped buzzing and clung to the undersides of the leaves. The wind ceased blowing and an awesome stillness was upon the land. She looked around and plugged on.

After a long struggle that seemed to be getting her nowhere, she decided to climb a tree again and take stock of her position. She should have been at the mound.

The bay was still empty. The storm clouds were rolling over the ground, but the mound was not to be seen. She climbed higher. In the opposite direction from which she had been walking stood the tree-covered rise.

A bird screamed almost in her ear. She shook her head, leaped to the ground and plugged back along her trail. The mire at her feet released stinky bubbles of methane gas.

Learning from her mistake, she climbed trees frequently now to make sure she was on the correct course. Presently there were smaller roots, smaller trees and, at last, she came out of the mangrove forest and stood on the edge of an empty canal. On the other side was the Indian mound. She ran full speed for it.

At its base grew more mangroves, but she barely noticed them in her excitement and relief. Whacking a path up the slope with her machete, she noticed, after a short climb, that the trees had changed. Mangroves gave way to figs, hardwoods and pines, trees of higher ground. That was encouraging, for she was above the flood mark. Burden thrust her head out of her shell and began digging the air.

At last on the summit, Billie Wind put her down and shinnied up another tree. An innocent landscape awash in a soft veil of clouds stretched out in beauty before her. She clung to the trunk for a long while, enchanted by the drowsy peacefulness of the scene.

A leaf stirred, then another and another.

"Here it comes," she said and slid down the tree to search for a hiding place behind a log or tree where she could pitch her sail and make a tent. Then a powerful gust struck her and almost knocked her over, and she knew a fragile tent would not do. Hurricanes, she remembered, could rip up trees and hurl them through the air like toothpicks.

She must dig into the ground. Make a burrow. And she must dig on the lee side of the mound out of the direct blast of the wind. She took out the adz, found a treeless spot about ten feet below the summit and dug.

The first drops of rain struck. They were like cold needles.

"What are you doing here?"

Billie Wind rolled her eyes and looked at Burden.

"What are you doing here?" The turtle's voice was croaky like a frog's.

"Forgive me, Charlie Wind, forgive me. The animals *really* do talk." A pair of running shoes stepped into her peripheral vision. She got slowly to her feet, her eyes following the shoes to the pants, the pants to the shirt, the shirt to the black eyes of an Indian boy. The eyes were wide and frightened, but he held his chin high and his shoulders did not tremble.

"Digging," she finally answered and dropped to her knees. Then she stood up again, reached out and touched him. He was real. He had real cheeks, eyelashes, teeth, fingernails and his breath came and went softly.

"What are *you* doing here?" she asked.

"I'm on my name-seeking quest; my puberty rites." His face grew solemn, and he pressed his full lips tightly against his teeth. "I am out adventuring to get a new name."

"You're alone?"

"Yes."

A limb cracked overhead and he glanced into the trees. Leaves twisted and spun on their stems. "Looks like a bad storm."

"It is. The bay is empty of water. That means hurricane." She pulled her machete out of her belt and handed it to the boy.

"Dig," she said. "We've got to make a shelter."

He dropped to his knees and brought the implement down with a smart blow. Billie Wind raked out the shells he had loosened with her adz. Glancing at each other, they set a rhythm and went to work, he striking, she hoeing. When they were three feet into the mound, the shells moved, slid, and the cave collapsed.

"Now what do we do?" the boy asked, rocking back on his heels. He wore his hair shoulder length and tied with a red thong around his head. His clothes were blue jeans and a Spider-Man T-shirt. A Windbreaker was tucked in his belt at his hip.

"Dig," she said and went back to work. He swung the machete without further comment. Billie Wind glanced over her shoulder at him. If he was scared he did not show it.

They dug more carefully now, packing the roof as they tunneled.

"We'll cover the entrance with my sail," she said. "By the way, what day is it?"

"It's the third week in September."

She counted in her head while she hoed out the shells, then whistled a low note. "Twelve weeks. I've been paddling around in this wilderness for twelve weeks."

"What for?"

A section of the ceiling started crumbling and she could not answer.

"What's your name?" she asked when she had stopped the rain of shells.

"Oats," he answered. "Oats Tiger."

She was about to laugh when she thought better of it. After all, her name was pretty funny, too.

"My name's Billie Wind." He did not laugh or comment, just nodded and dug. Presently he sat back on his heels.

"Billie Wind? Did you say Billie Wind?" She shook her head "yes."

"Then you must be the girl the Panther Paw tribe is looking for. Word went out through the medicine men to watch the rivers for a girl in a dugout. Some bulldozer operators said they saw her heading toward the Fahkahatchee. Is that you?"

She did not answer immediately. The wind-gusted rain stung her face and thoughts of Charlie Wind and Mamau Whispering Wind swept over her.

She shook her head to forget. There was no time for self-pity now. She must dig and dig furiously. Billie Wind concentrated her thoughts on her new friend.

"Oats," she said. "Well, that's an easy name to remember."

"It's a dumb name," he snapped. "That's why I'm here. I'm only twelve; not really old enough for an adventure to find a new name. But I don't want to be called Oats anymore, so I persuaded my mother to let me go.

"I've been gone for three days." He paused. "The forecast was sun, with stormy weather next week."

"What name would you like?"

"I don't know. But the council will know when I come

home and tell them I found the nest of a rare Everglades kite, tracked a wild cat and . . . dug a shelter from a hurricane." He cast the machete deep.

"They named my brother Cattle Jumper after he stopped a stampede up north of Lake Okeechobee. Maybe they'll call me Machete Joe." He drove the long blade into the ground.

"Watch out!" he shouted. "It's collapsing." They threw their backs against the ceiling, but gravity was relentless. The shells cascaded like water and filled the shelter.

"Now what?" Billie Wind asked. "We've got to crawl under tree roots or do something. The wind will blow us away."

"I'll lash us to a tree with my belt."

"We'll sail off with the tree."

She squatted on the ground, wondering if they would have time to cut off the limbs of a fig tree and lash them together. Fig trees sent down hundreds of roots from their limbs deep into the ground. They would hold even under the worst blows. They could wedge themselves between the roots and limbs and wrap up in the sail. But was there time?

The rain was falling steadily now and turning into spray as stout winds gusted it. Billie Wind's hand touched a chunk of limestone shells fused by water and time. She rolled to her knees and hands.

"A huge hunk of rock," she said. "We can dig under it. It won't collapse." She picked up her adz and crawled to its downhill side.

"Oats! Oats! There's already a cave here." Lying flat on her belly she wiggled her head and shoulders under the rock and looked into a dark room. From far in the back came a hiss.

"Snakes," she called.

"I'm not afraid of snakes," he answered. "Go on in. I'm following." He threw himself down on his belly and caterpillared forward.

"Snake Tiger," he said. "I like that. A snake pit is a good place to hide. It will be dry even in a storm. Snakes don't like to get wet when they sleep."

Billie Wind backed out to get Burden and her deerskin pouch. Coming down the slope, she stepped in a hole beside the limestone rock. It avalanched and carried her into the cave. She was looking at a flat ledge just above her shoulder.

Hissst. Taking her penknife in hand she raised her arm. When her eyes adjusted to the dim light she could make out a low room tilted upward. She was pleased to see that. Water would not collect on the slope. She felt the ground. It was dry.

Hissst. She studied the ledge near the ceiling.

"Are you all right?" Oats called, wiggling his way in.

Two eyes gleamed from the ledge and she dared not answer. She had not heard snakes. She had heard a panther.

A soft purr of recognition vibrated the shelter and the smudge-faced Florida panther came out of the shadows and crouched in a squat.

"Coootchobee!" She reached for him. "I'd know you anywhere with that snub face." She patted his big paw and rubbed his forehead. "Hello, hello." He rubbed her with his head in greeting.

"Either I have paddled in a circle and am back in the Fahkahatchee Strand, or you have taken your long trek away from your home to settle down on your own territory." She studied him. "I think you're on your own."

The panther licked his paw and washed his face.

"Oats," she whispered. "Come here. Meet my old friend Coootchobee, the panther."

She could hear the shells clatter as he wedged his way toward her.

"A panther?" His voice was tense. She grabbed his hand and pulled him up the incline until he could dig in his shoes and sit up. His jaw was clenched bravely. He did not whimper. Outside the wind whistled as it drove the rain horizontally through the air.

"Listen," said Billie Wind. A low rumble sounded from far away. It slowly grew louder, as if some comet were approaching the earth.

"Tidal wave. It's coming."

Oats moved closer to Billie Wind and the panther. Taking a deep breath, he turned his head until he was looking at Coootchobee.

"He's beautiful," he said, licking his fear-dried lips.

Billie Wind was no longer thinking of Coootchobee. The sound of the sea returning held her spellbound. It moaned like a being. Oats heard and shivered. The air was icy cold. Billie Wind snuggled closer to warm Coootchobee and gave Oats the sail to wrap himself in.

They watched the entranceway. Nothing could be seen but a wall of solid rain. Hours passed. The sun set, and they were in darkness.

Presently Oats lifted his head from his knees.

"The waves are smashing the bottom of the mound. What a tide!"

"We're okay," she said reassuringly. "Coootchobee is not worried; and he knows a lot. Charlie Wind once told me we must keep the animals on Earth, for they know everything: how to keep warm, predict the storms, live in darkness or blazing sun, how to navigate the skies, to organize societies, how to make chemicals and fireproof skins. The animals know the Earth as we do not."

All through the night and the small hours of the morning, Billie Wind and Oats sat still and listened. The cave grew warm with their body heat, and Coootchobee panted in his sleep.

At last the cave brightened. The sun had come over the horizon and was sending its light through the storm clouds into the cave.

"We made it so far," whispered Oats and stretched out his cramped legs. The panther lifted his head.

"Hello," Oats said hoarsely to the sleek beast.

Coootchobee raised his lips and wrinkled his nose. He held the warning expression.

"Oats is all right," Billie Wind said to the irritated panther and stroked his flat head.

The lips remained lifted.

"He likes you," Billie Wind said.

"He doesn't look like it."

"He hasn't showed his canine teeth. Just lifting his lips and wrinkling his nose means you get a passing grade."

"I want an A," Oats said. "How do I get that?" He sat perfectly still.

Presently Coootchobee lowered his lip, closed his mouth and put his head on his paw, and as he did so, Billie Wind heard a soft expulsion of air.

"Pheww." It was Oats letting out his breath.

The waves continued to boom at the bottom of the mound most of the morning. Then they climbed higher, sending salt spray into the air. The wind sounds increased. The rain deluged the mound.

"We are nearing the height of the storm," Oats said in a low voice. The waves crashed constantly.

"I'm hungry," said Billie Wind. "Want a piece of fish?"

"I can't eat. I must fast like my forefathers did."

"But you need your strength."

"I have strength." He wrapped his arms around his knees as Billie Wind unwrapped the fish and ate.

"I would cheat if I were you."

"I want a new name."

The rain sounded like bullets hitting the earth; the wind shrieked and whistled.

Billie Wind glanced down at Burden. She was halfway into the floor of the den, digging slowly and skillfully as if nothing were happening.

"That turtle is fearless," she said. "She has to be. She carries the Earth on her back."

"You believe that?"

She did not answer. The storm had reached its height, and they were both afraid.

So Spoke Burden
and All of the Animals

Sometime before noon the voice of the wind lowered and the waves boomed far away. Half asleep, half awake, Billie Wind heard the change and glanced at Oats. He was still hugging his knees, his eyes wide open.

"Hear that?" she whispered.

"Yes," he answered. "The worst is over."

Coootchobee heard the change, too. He lifted his tawny head, and twisted his ears and listened. Then he yawned, curling his red tongue to the roof of his mouth. His pointed teeth were very white. Billie Wind thought about his presence here on the mound.

"Are we near the Fahkahatchee Strand?" she asked Oats.

"Ten or fifteen miles."

"Very close for an animal that travels twice that far every night."

"Why?"

"I must have paddled backward farther than I thought," she answered. "I last saw Coootchobee on the Fahkahatchee Strand. Where are we?"

"My village is not far from this mound on the Chobee River." He paused. "I hope everyone got to high land. We get hurricane warnings. I am sure my clan went to Naples or the Highway village, where the land is higher.

"I hope my brother went. He was always saying how he would stay home if a hurricane hit so that he could see what it was like.

"I hope he took my Sony TV and the Chris-Craft. They wouldn't survive this. My village is low. Right on the water. But everyone knows what to do."

Oats talked on and on. His fears gone, his life intact, he was thinking about other people.

"Billie Wind," he finally said. "I was afraid. Is that terrible?"

"So was I," she answered. "But it's smart to be afraid sometimes. We are alive because our ancestors were afraid of the hurricanes and built mounds and villages above the storm tides."

"But—Coootchobee. How did you dare go into a panther's den not knowing who he was? That scared me worse than the wind and rain."

"I had no choice. I was avalanched in, but when I saw his face I knew all was going to turn out all right. I saved Coootchobee's life. Now he has saved mine." She rubbed her chin. "That sounds like an old Indian legend, doesn't it?"

Oats nodded and crept down the incline to the den entrance. He thrust his head out.

"Sun!" he called. "The sun is out. Wow, it's wonderful." Billie Wind slid to the entrance and wiggled into the sunlight right behind Oats. She stood up and lifted her arms.

"It's a beautiful summer day. The sky is clear, the sea is blue, the air is warm."

"We must be in the eye of the storm," Oats said. "This must be the hole in the center of the whirling clouds that the weathermen talk about. It's really beautiful; but it's a tease. There's more to come."

Billie Wind ran to the top of the mound. Uprooted trees lay like giant clubs down its side.

"Everything has been destroyed," she whispered uncomfortably.

"Scary," added Oats. "Not even my leather belt would have held us. We would have been blown to our deaths for sure."

After a short time, the clouds covered the sun and circled counterclockwise.

"Here comes the other side of the storm," Oats said. "We're not out of it yet."

The first shower of rain hit the ground as they wiggled back into the den. Coootchobee lifted his head as they came sprawling in.

"Why didn't you get up to see the sun?" Billie Wind asked him. "Did you know the storm was not over? I think you did. I think the pressure of the air tells you."

Oats crawled up on the ledge away from Coootchobee and stretched out. Presently Billie Wind heard the boy's quiet breathing that told her he was, at last, at ease. The den grew dark. The rain washed down again.

"Oats?"

"What?"

"Do you think the animal gods talk?"

"No."

"I do."

"That's silly. That's just old legends."

"Coootchobee spoke to you."

"Coootchobee spoke to me?"

"He said as plain as he could: 'The storm is not over.' "

Oats thought about that. "That's true. He didn't go out. And that sort of said, 'Why get up when there's more to come?' "

The wind shrieked again and the rain pelted the leaves on the ground; but there was no tidal wave. The fury had gone out of the storm. The sea was back in its bed and could barely be heard as it beat on the shores of the bay. The constant sound put them all to sleep.

Billie Wind awoke in the late afternoon and lay on her back listening to a gentle swish of the rain. She could not hear the wind. Slowly she rolled to her knees and sat up. Burden was in her burrow. Coootchobee was stretched on his side, his eyes open. Oats was still sleeping.

She put her ear to the ground. The turtle was scratching and digging deeper and deeper into the earth.

"I hear what you are saying, Burden. At last, I hear your message. It's the Earth that matters. Not the stars or the comets, but the plain old Earth. And you are right. It's all we've got. Dig it lovingly."

She dozed off again, dreaming not of the galaxies and her distant star, but of grass blades and otters and pure clear water.

The next thing she knew Oats was shouting from the top of the mound.

"The sun! Here it comes again." She slid out the den entrance and ran up the hill to his side, laughing excitedly. Then she became quiet as she looked down on the bay, the islands, the Gulf of Mexico. Not a leaf remained on the once-green mangroves. They had been ripped off by the hundred-mile-an-hour wind and the pounding salt tide. Cast among the trees were boards, splintered boats, seaweed, dead fish, house tops and birds. Billie Wind put her hands to her mouth. The destruction before her was awesome.

"Looks like a nuclear bomb hit it," said Oats. "Nothing is left." He shuddered.

"I heard the turtle speak today," Billie Wind said.

"The turtle speak?" Oats scratched his head. "What did she say?"

"That we must love the Earth or it will look like this."

"What else did she say?"

"That life can be destroyed unless we work at saving it."

"That's true. But, hey, look we survived." He turned his hands palms up, closed them, opened them and held them close to his face.

"I lived through a hurricane."

"I know your new name," Billie Wind said.

"What is it?"

"Hurricane Tiger."

He turned his head quickly and smiled at her.

"I like it. I like it." Throwing his arms above his head he shouted to the clearing sky.

"Hurricane Tiger is my name."

Billie Wind went back for her pouch, took out the fish and coconut and placed it on top of the mound. She sat down.

"Hurricane Tiger," she said, passing the food to him. "Eat up."

He laughed proudly and sat down beside her.

"By the way," Hurricane said, "what *are* you doing here? You never answered my question."

"I'm on punishment."

"On punishment?"

"Yes." She took a bite of a tuber. "For not believing

in the serpents in the pa-hay-okee, or the little men who live underground—or the animal gods who talk."

"You're on punishment for that?"

She nodded.

"That's terrible." He frowned. "No one believes that stuff anymore."

"I do."

Hurricane Tiger swallowed his fish and stared at her. He studied her nose, the curve of her cheeks, the sweep of her high forehead to see if there was some hole in her head.

"Do you really?" he finally asked.

"I have seen them; and I have heard what they have to say."

"What do they have to say?"

She leaned her elbows on her knees and looked out at the sea.

"They say there is no other planet in all the universe with turtles and panthers and saw grass upon it. There are no spacemen, no Martians, no people of the constellations. Just us."

"The animals say that we are the only planet with life?"

"Yes, we are alone in the universe."

"In the universe? But there must be another Earth somewhere. The odds are . . ."

"Are what?"

"That there is another planet like ours."

"Have you ever seen two leaves alike, two flowers,

two fish, two panthers, two turtles . . . two pa-hay-okees?"

Oats shook his head.

"Two yous? Two mes?"

Hurricane Tiger pondered that.

"We have lots to do, then," he said.

Billie Wind closed her deerskin pouch and slung it over her shoulder. She looked back at the destruction and started down the mound.

"Where are you going?" Hurricane called.

"Home," she said. "I have heard what the animals have to say."

"Wait; I'm going, too." He led the way.

As Billie Wind climbed over fallen trees and broken limbs she saw smoke rising from the Indian village on the river. Hurricane's tribe had come back to restore their homes and begin again.

And, at last, she understood Charlie Wind. He had sent her on a mission, not a punishment. Spider lilies were lightning bolts and lightning bolts were spider lilies. Albert Einstein had said the same thing in physics, $E = mc^2$, but that had been destructive. So it must be said in spider lilies.

"And oh, that will be beautiful, Charlie Wind. The Earth will not blow up and die."

ABOUT THE AUTHOR

JEAN CRAIGHEAD GEORGE was born in Washington, D.C., and was graduated from Penn State University. She has traveled widely and written many children's books, in which she blends a profound respect for nature with a deep understanding of the reciprocal relationship between the human and the natural. Her other books include JULIE OF THE WOLVES, which was awarded the 1973 Newbery Medal; THE CRY OF THE CROW; GOING TO THE SUN; and ONE DAY IN THE DESERT.